FUN學

美國英語閱讀課本

各學科實用課文 二版

AMERICAN SCHOOL TEXTBOOK

READING KEY

5

Workbook

作者 Michael A. Putlack & e-Creative Contents 譯者 丁宥暄

01 What Is a Globe?

A Listen to the passage and fill in the blanks. 🎧 37

Look around your classroom. You can _____ see a globe in it. What is a _____? A globe is a _____ of the earth that shows what the earth looks like.

A globe is a kind of _____. It shows _____ _____ the land and water on the earth. You can turn a globe and see all seven _____ and five oceans. But that is not all _____ a globe shows.

Look _____ at the globe. There are many _____ on it. Some are horizontal lines while others are _____ lines. These lines on the _____ are two sets of imaginary lines that _____ the earth.

The horizontal lines that circle from east to west are lines of _____. The vertical lines that circle from north to south are lines of _____. The lines of longitude _____ _____ the North Pole and the South Pole. When we know the latitude and longitude _____ a place, we know its _____ location on the globe.

B Write the meaning of each word or phrase from Word List (main book p.104) in English.

1	或許	_____	7	虛構的;假想的 _____
2	地球儀	_____	8	緯線 _____
3	模型	_____	9	經線 _____
4	仔細地	_____	10	通過 _____
5	而;然而	_____	11	北極 _____
6	格子;座標方格 _____	12	南極 _____

Daily Test 02 Understanding Hemispheres

A **A** Listen to the passage and fill in the blanks. 🎧 38

_____ divide the earth into four different hemispheres. They are the Northern, Southern, Western, and Eastern _____. The word "hemi" means "_____." A hemisphere covers _____ one half of the earth.

The earth is divided into the Northern and _____ hemispheres by the equator. The _____ is the line of latitude that lies in the middle of the earth. _____ the equator is the Northern Hemisphere. Asia, _____, and North America are in it. _____ the equator is the Southern Hemisphere. It _____ parts of Africa and South America. Australia and _____ are in it, too.

The earth is divided into the _____ and Western hemispheres by the prime meridian. The _____ _____ is a line of longitude that goes from the North Pole to the South Pole. It goes directly through _____, England. North and South America are in the _____ Hemisphere. Europe, Asia, Africa, _____, and Antarctica are in the Eastern Hemisphere.

B Write the meaning of each word or phrase from Word List in English.

1 地理學家 _____
2 半球 _____
3 北半球 _____
4 南半球 _____
5 西半球 _____

6 東半球 _____
7 包含 _____
8 正好地；確切地 _____
9 赤道 _____
10 本初子午線 _____

A Listen to the passage and fill in the blanks. 🎧39

The states in the West are all near the _____ Ocean. They are California, _____, Oregon, and Washington. Alaska and Hawaii are in the western _____, but they do not touch any other _____.

The states in the West are known for their long _____ along the Pacific, lush forests, hot deserts, and _____ mountains.

The West has a _____ of climates. Nevada and California have many _____. Death Valley, California, is one of the _____ places on the planet. But there are also many places that get _____ _____ rain. In fact, even _____ _____ are found in Oregon and Washington. The western climate sometimes can be very _____. Earthquakes often _____ along the Pacific coast. There are active volcanoes in Alaska, _____, and Washington.

The West has _____ natural resources. There is plenty of _____ soil for farming. The forests provide much _____ wood throughout the country. The West is also a region of low _____ and tall mountains. The Cascade Range and Sierra Nevada Mountains are all located in the West.

B Write the meaning of each word or phrase from Word List in English.

1	接觸；碰到	_____	7	活火山	_____
2	海岸線	_____	8	眾多的；非常多的	_____
3	蒼翠茂盛的	_____	9	很多的	_____
4	崎嶇不平的	_____	10	（土地）肥沃的	_____
5	各式各樣的	_____	11	珍貴的	_____
6	極端的	_____	12	遍及	_____

04 The California Gold Rush

🎧 40

A Listen to the passage and fill in the blanks.

James Marshall was a _____ who was hired at Sutter's Mill in California.

In _____, he was building a mill _____ the American River for John

Sutter. One day, while working on the mill, Marshall found some _____ of a

shiny metal in the river. He and John Sutter tried to keep this discovery a

_____. However, _____ soon started to spread, and then everyone

knew there was _____ in California.

It took _____ for people in the East to hear the news. But, soon,

_____ of people had moved to California. By 1849, more than 80,000

people had _____ to California. They were all _____ for gold. This

was the California _____ _____. People called these gold _____

"forty-niners" because they arrived in California in _____. Some _____

gold and became rich. Others found nothing and left empty _____.

During the early _____, the West was a quiet region with a small

_____. However, the discovery of gold changed the West into a land

with _____ cities. The population also _____, and California

became a state in 1850.

B Write the meaning of each word or phrase from Word List in English.

1 木匠　　　_____

2 雇用　　　_____

3 磨坊　　　_____

4 小薄片　　_____

5 祕密　　　_____

6 謠言；傳聞　_____

7 湧現；衝；蜂擁前往　_____

8 淘金潮　　_____

9 四九人；淘金客　_____

10 空手的；一無所有的　_____

11 忙亂的；熙攘的　_____

12 激增；迅速擴大　_____

05 The Environment of the Southwest

The Southwest is famous for its sunny climate and _____ landforms. _____, New Mexico, Oklahoma, and Texas are the four _____ in the Southwest.

Much of the _____ is hot and dry. So many parts of the land are covered by _____. The Painted Desert and Sonoran Desert are _____ in Arizona.

But it still has many different _____ features. The Rocky Mountains _____ _____ the Southwest. There are also many plateaus, canyons, mesas, and _____. The Colorado Plateau is the major _____ found in the Southwest. The area is famous for its _____. The Grand Canyon is one _____ _____.

While much of the land is dry, there are _____ some major rivers in the Southwest. The _____ River flows through Arizona. It actually _____ the Grand Canyon. The _____ _____ River is another major river. It flows _____ Texas and Mexico.

B Write the meaning of each word or phrase from Word List in English.

1	以……著名	_____	7	穿過	_____
2	氣候	_____	8	高原	_____
3	不平常的；奇特的	_____	9	峽谷	_____
4	地形	_____	10	臺地	_____
5	地理學的；地理的	_____	11	孤峰	_____
6	特徵；特色	_____	12	流經	_____

06 The Economy of the Southwest

A Listen to the passage and fill in the blanks. 🎧 42

Although the Southwest gets little _____, it is rich in natural resources.
Two of the most important resources are found _____ the ground. They are
_____ and oil.

Minerals such as coal, copper, silver, and _____ are mined in Texas,
Arizona, and New Mexico. Texas and Oklahoma are two of the largest
_____ of oil. Oil is a common name for _____. It is also
_____ "black gold" since it is so valuable. "Black gold" has helped build
the _____ economy. The oil found in the Southwest is used
_____ the United States.

Today, the states in the Southwest have _____ economies. Every year,
more and more Americans move to the _____. The reason is that there
are many different _____ in the Southwest.

The _____ _____ continues to be a big business in the Southwest.
The _____ industry is big there, too. Trade and _____
industries, such as aircraft production, also help the Southwest grow.

B Write the meaning of each word or phrase from Word List in English.

1 降雨；降雨量 _____
2 在……下面 _____
3 開採（礦物） _____
4 石油 _____
5 給……取綽號 _____

6 興旺的；繁榮的 _____
7 石油工業 _____
8 石油化學工業 _____
9 高科技的 _____
10 飛機；航空器總稱 _____

07 The Environment of the Southeast

One of the largest _____ in the United States is the Southeast. It includes _____ states. They are Alabama, Arkansas, Florida, Georgia, Kentucky, _____, Mississippi, North Carolina, South Carolina, _____, Virginia, and West Virginia.

_____ is a large part of the region's economy. Because of its location, the Southeast has a warm climate for _____ _____ the year. The heavy rainfall and fertile soil there help _____ grow a variety of crops. Its long _____ season also makes the Southeast a _____ of many fruits and vegetables.

The Southeast has many rivers, lakes, and _____. The _____ River flows through the western part of the Southeast. The Mississippi River has been at the center of travel and trade in the country for _____ _____ years.

There are also many valuable natural resources _____ the region. Much of the coal used in the _____ country is mined in West Virginia and _____.

B | Write the meaning of each word or phrase from Word List in English.

1 地區 _____
2 農業 _____
3 經濟 _____
4 位置；地點 _____
5 農作物；莊稼 _____
6 生長季 _____
7 來源 _____
8 溼地 _____

08 The Civil Rights Movement

A Listen to the passage and fill in the blanks. 🎧44

In the _____, most people in the Southeast farmed. There were many _____. Plantation owners grew _____ _____ that they could sell to make money. _____ was the most important cash crop.

Plantations _____ many workers, so many _____ owned slaves. These slaves were black _____. Their _____ were very difficult.

Meanwhile, _____ was illegal in most Northern states. Many _____ believed that slavery was wrong and should be ended. In the _____, the North and South _____ the Civil War. The North won, and slavery became _____.

However, most _____ in the South still did not have the same rights as _____ citizens. There was a lot of _____. Blacks could not live together, work together, or _____ use the same _____ with whites.

In the 1950s, the _____ _____ Movement began. Martin Luther King, Jr. became one of its _____. He led _____ demanding equal treatment for all people. Finally, in _____, the Civil Rights Act was passed. It _____ that everyone would be treated equally.

B Write the meaning of each word or phrase from Word List in English.

1 1800 年代 _____

2 大農場 _____

3 經濟作物（如菸草、棉花等） _____

4 美國南方人 _____

5 同時 _____

6 奴隸制度 _____

7 非法的 _____

8 美國北方人 _____

9 美國內戰；南北戰爭（1861–1865） _____

10 種族隔離 _____

11 盥洗室；廁所 _____

12 美國民權運動 _____

13 抗議 _____

14 要求 _____

15 平等待遇 _____

16 擔保；保證 _____

09 The Environment of the Northeast

A Listen to the passage and fill in the blanks. 🎧 45

The Northeast is divided into two _____: New England and the Middle _____ States. The New England states are Maine, _____ _____, Massachusetts, Vermont, Rhode Island, and Connecticut. The Middle Atlantic States are New York, Pennsylvania, _____ _____, Delaware, and Maryland.

Along the Atlantic coast, there are many _____, capes, and islands. Cape Cod, Massachusetts, is one of the most famous _____ in the Northeast. The Atlantic _____ Plain has many deep harbors. Cities with _____ can easily trade with other regions and countries. So, the Northeast cities, such as New York, Boston, and Philadelphia, have become important _____ centers.

There are many mountain _____, too. The Appalachian Mountains are _____ in almost every state in the Northeast. The _____ are one of the oldest mountain ranges in the world.

The Northeastern states enjoy four _____ seasons. So they can be very hot in summer but very cold in _____. In fall, the colorful _____ is a well-known feature of the Northeast's _____.

B Write the meaning of each word or phrase from Word List in English.

1 （區以下的）分區 _____   6 山脈 _____ c
2 海灣 _____   7 山脈 _____ r
3 岬；海角 _____   8 明顯的；清楚的 _____
4 大西洋沿岸平原 _____   9 葉子 _____
5 貿易中心 _____   10 著名的 _____

10 The Leading Industries of the Northeast

A Listen to the passage and fill in the blanks. 🎧 46

Many of the first _____ from Europe settled in the Northeast. Many were _____. In the mid _____, most Americans lived and worked on farms. However, from the late 1700s to the mid _____, the Industrial Revolution changed _____ _____ people lived.

Machines _____ hand tools, and goods were produced faster. New industries were _____, and the economy expanded. _____ soon became as important as farms.

As the Industrial _____ spread across the country, the Northeast became the center of the country's _____ industry. All of the new factories and _____ needed many workers. So, more and more _____ came to New York looking for new _____.

_____ on size, the Northeast is the smallest _____ in the U.S. However, it is big in many _____. The Northeast has more _____ areas than any other region. Education is also very important in the _____. Excellent schools like _____, Yale, and MIT are there. New York City is the world's leading _____ center. Also, the airports and _____ all over the Northeast help import and _____ huge amounts of goods.

B Write the meaning of each word or phrase from Word List in English.

1	殖民者	_____	
2	定居；移居於	_____	
3	工業革命	_____	
4	取代	_____	
5	用手操作的簡易工具	_____	
6	擴張；擴大	_____	
7	金融的	_____	
8	移民	_____	
9	根據……；基於……	_____	
10	大都市的	_____	
11	機場	_____	
12	港；港口	_____	

11 The Midwest Region

Listen to the passage and fill in the blanks. 🎧47

The Midwest region is _____ _____ _____ 12 states. They are Ohio, Indiana, _____, Wisconsin, Illinois, Minnesota, _____, Missouri, North Dakota, South Dakota, Nebraska, and Kansas.

The Midwest is made up of low, flat _____. The major landforms are the two _____ plains: the Central Plains and the Great _____. Also, three important _____ run through it. They are the _____ Mississippi River, the Ohio River, and the _____ River. The _____ _____ are also in the Midwest.

The Midwest has two _____ industries: farming and manufacturing. The Midwest is called the "_____ of America." It has _____ fields of wheat, corn, and other crops. Also, many Midwestern farmers raise _____, cows, and other _____. Much of America's food comes from the _____.

The Midwest is also a _____ center. Henry Ford started building cars in _____, Michigan. Detroit quickly became the _____ center of the world. Several large car _____ have factories there. There are also many other industries all _____ the Midwest.

Write the meaning of each word or phrase from Word List in English.

1 由……組成　　_____
2 平坦的　　_____
3 內陸平原　　_____
4 巨大的；浩瀚的　　_____
5 北美五大湖　　_____

6 糧倉；糧產區　　_____
7 無數的　　_____
8 小麥　　_____
9 （總稱）家畜　　_____
10 汽車　　_____

12 The Mountain States

A Listen to the passage and fill in the blanks. 🎧 48

Idaho, Montana, _____, Colorado, and Utah are the five _____ in the Mountain States region.

The Mountain States are _____ with mountains. The _____ Rocky Mountains run through them. The Continental Divide _____ north to south along the _____ of the Rockies. These states also have many rivers and _____ forests. Great Salt Lake is located in _____ Utah. It is the largest _____ body of salt water in the Western Hemisphere.

_____ is one of the most important industries in the Mountain States. The _____ Mountains provide plenty of metal and mineral resources, such as _____ and natural gas.

_____ is another important industry in the Mountain States. Outdoor _____, such as skiing, mountain climbing, and rafting, _____ thousands of tourists every year.

The population of the Mountain States is _____ low. Few cities have populations greater than _____. Denver and Salt Lake City are the region's _____ cities.

B Write the meaning of each word or phrase from Word List in English.

1 被……覆蓋 _____
2 雄偉的；壯觀的 _____
3 大陸分水嶺 _____
4 山峰 _____
5 落磯山脈 _____
6 內陸的；內地的 _____
7 採礦；礦業 _____
8 觀光業；旅遊業 _____
9 戶外的 _____
10 消遣；娛樂 _____
11 泛舟 _____
12 吸引 _____
13 遊客；觀光客 _____
14 很；相當 _____

13 How Do Animals Grow?

Every animal has a _____ _____. Just as there are many _____ kinds of animals, there are many kinds of life cycles.

Almost all animals come from _____ eggs. Many birds lay _____ in nests. Fish and _____ lay eggs in the water. _____ also lay eggs. They hatch from eggs outside a _____ body. After hatching, some animals, such as _____ and insects, go through complete body changes before they become _____.

Mammals begin their _____ inside their mothers. They _____ from fertilized eggs inside their mothers' bodies. They are born _____. When they are born, they are _____ but look a lot like the adults. As they grow, they get larger, and their _____ change. However, they do not _____ _____ other major changes. This kind of _____ is called direct development.

Animals also develop at different _____. A _____ ____ becomes an adult in about 10 days. A dog becomes an adult at about three _____ of age.

B Write the meaning of each word or phrase from Word List in English.

1	生命週期	_____	8	孵化	_____
2	使受精	_____	9	雌性	_____
3	受精卵	_____	10	經歷	_____
4	產卵；下蛋	_____	11	極小的；微小的	_____
5	巢；窩	_____	12	看起來像……	_____
6	兩棲動物	_____	13	速度	_____
7	爬蟲類動物	_____	14	果蠅	

14 What Is Metamorphosis?

Listen to the passage and fill in the blanks. 🎧 50

Animals go through _____ as they live and grow. Some animals, _____ _____ fish and people, just get _____ as they grow older. However, some animals _____ big life cycle changes called metamorphosis.

Metamorphosis means a major change in the _____ _____ of an animal. Butterflies and _____ undergo metamorphosis. Most amphibians, such as frogs, also go through _____.

There are four _____ in complete metamorphosis. Let's look closely at the metamorphosis of a _____.

First, a butterfly _____ a fertilized egg. In the second stage, a tiny _____, or larva, hatches from the egg. The caterpillar begins eating and growing to _____ _____ the next stage. In the third stage, it _____ a cocoon. This is a hard shell that the caterpillar makes by _____ threads around _____ so that it becomes a pupa. Inside the _____, it undergoes a metamorphosis. At last, in the _____ stage, the adult butterfly comes _____ _____ the cocoon.

Write the meaning of each word or phrase from Word List in English.

1 經歷 _____
2 （動物的）變態 _____
3 蝴蝶 _____
4 蛾 _____
5 階段；時期 _____

6 毛毛蟲 _____
7 幼蟲；幼體 _____
8 繭 _____
9 吐絲 _____
10 蛹 _____

15 How Do Animals Respond to Changes?

A Listen to the passage and fill in the blanks. 🎧 51

_____ often change. Animals _____ to changes in their environment in different ways.

Animals often _____ _____ their instincts. _____ is something animals are born with. For instance, they might _____ which animals are dangerous and which ones are not. Also, a _____ knows how to _____ a web to catch food.

Many animals have _____ to winter by migrating or hibernating. When the weather gets cold, some animals _____ to warmer places in search of food. Some animals, like bears, find places to _____. Since its body is _____ working, a hibernating animal does not need much energy, so it does not need to eat _____ the winter. Migration and hibernation are both _____ behaviors.

Some animals also have learned _____. Mammal mothers usually teach their young _____ behaviors. They teach their _____ how to get food and how to protect _____. Bear _____ learn to climb trees at about six _____. Most _____ behavior is learned.

B Write the meaning of each word or phrase from Word List in English.

1 環境　　_____
2 對……作出反應　_____
3 依賴；依靠　_____
4 本能；天性　_____
5 蜘蛛　_____
6 （蜘蛛、蠶等）吐絲；結（繭）　_____
7 織網　_____
8 適應　_____

9 遷徙 (v.)　_____
10 冬眠 (v.)　_____
11 幾乎不　_____
12 遷徙 (n.)　_____
13 冬眠 (n.)　_____
14 行為；態度　_____
15 幼獸；幼禽　_____
16 （熊、獅、虎等的）幼獸　_____

16 Animal Adaptations for Survival

A Listen to the passage and fill in the blanks. 🎧 52

Animals have various _____ that help them survive. An adaptation might be a body part or behavior that an _____ gets from its parents.

Frogs and _____ have long tongues that help them catch insects. Lions have great speed, strength, and sharp _____ and _____ to hunt their food.

Many animals have body _____ or shapes that match their _____. _____ is a good example. Animals in _____ areas often have white fur. Animals in forests often have brown _____. Some animals, like _____, can even change colors frequently to match their environment. When these animals stay _____, a predator may not see them.

Some animals use mimicry to _____ being eaten by other animals. _____ is looking like another organism or object. The _____ looks like a stone. The wings of the gray butterfly have _____ that look like eyes of an _____. The snake _____ caterpillar looks like a real snake.

B Write the meaning of each word or phrase from Word List in English.

1	適應	_____	9	常常；頻繁	_____
2	蜥蜴	_____	10	靜止的；不動的	_____
3	舌頭	_____	11	保持不動	_____
4	爪	_____	12	掠食者；食肉動物	_____
5	環境	_____	13	擬態	_____
6	偽裝；保護色	_____	14	石頭魚	_____
7	毛皮	_____	15	斑點	_____
8	變色龍	_____	16	善於模仿者	_____

17 What Changes Earth's Surface?

A Listen to the passage and fill in the blanks. 🎧53

Earth's _____ is changing all the time. Some _____ are very slow. Some changes _____ very quickly.

One kind of change is _____ by weathering. _____ is the process by which large rocks are broken down into small _____ for many years. Weathering can happen in many _____. _____ water and strong winds can weather rocks. Changing _____ and some chemicals can also weather rocks. Usually, weathering takes a very long time to _____.

_____ happens after weathering. It occurs when _____ rocks or soil are _____ away to other places. Typically, wind, water, and glaciers _____ erosion. Like weathering, erosion is often a slow _____. For example, it took the Colorado River _____ _____ years to make the Grand Canyon. This is _____ erosion. Wind erosion can _____ _____ valuable soil and make deserts. A _____ is a huge mass of moving ice. It moves _____ and other things in its path wherever it goes.

B Write the meaning of each word or phrase from Word List in English.

1	起因於…… _____	8	被風化的 _____
2	風化；風化作用 _____	9	帶走；搬走 _____
3	分解 _____	10	一般地；通常 _____
4	急衝的；急流的 _____	11	冰河 _____
5	使風化 _____	12	吹走 _____
6	化學物質 _____	13	塊；團；堆 _____
7	侵蝕；侵蝕作用 _____	14	路徑；軌道 _____

18 Fast Changes to Earth's Surface

🎧 54

A Listen to the passage and fill in the blanks.

Weathering and erosion usually take _____ _____ years to change Earth's surface. However, earthquakes, volcanoes, and other _____ weathers can change Earth's surface quickly.

An earthquake is the _____ of Earth's surface caused by the _____ movement of rock in the crust. _____ can cause great changes to the land. They can cause land to _____ or rise. They can _____ mountains and even change the _____ that rivers and streams follow.

Volcanoes can also _____ change Earth's surface. When a volcano _____, lava and other materials _____ onto Earth's surface. These materials _____ _____ to form a mountain. Many _____ volcanoes can even create _____ in the middle of Earth's oceans.

Hurricanes, tornadoes, and _____ can also change Earth's surface quickly. _____ cause strong winds and heavy rains. _____ are powerful windstorms that _____ most things in their paths. Floods carry away _____ and soil. These violent _____ of weather can change the land in just a few _____ or hours.

B Write the meaning of each word or phrase from Word List in English.

1 地震 _____
2 火山 _____
3 激烈的；猛烈的 _____
4 突然的；迅速的 _____
5 地殼 _____
6 倒塌；瓦解 _____

7 路線；路徑 _____
8 小河；溪流 _____
9 立即；馬上 _____
10 噴出；爆發 _____
11 熔岩 _____
12 逐漸堆積 _____

19 Our Solar System

A Listen to the passage and fill in the blanks.   ∩ 55

The _____ _____ is made up of the sun and all the _____ that orbit it. This includes planets, moons, and _____. The sun is the _____ object in our solar system.

The planets are divided into two _____: the inner planets and the _____ planets. The inner planets are the four planets _____ to the sun: Mercury, Venus, Earth, and _____. The outer planets are Jupiter, Saturn, _____, and Neptune. They are _____ away from the sun.

The inner planets all have _____ surfaces. They are _____ than the outer planets. None of the inner planets has more than two _____.

The outer planets are all huge and mostly made up of _____. They are often called gas _____. The outer planets all have many moons. They are also surrounded by _____ that are made of _____, ice, or rock.

The asteroid belt _____ the inner planets from the outer planets. It lies between _____ and Mars.

B Write the meaning of each word or phrase from Word List in English.

1 太陽系   _____
2 環繞（天體等的）軌道運行 _____
3 行星   _____
4 衛星   _____
5 小行星   _____
6 內行星   _____

7 外行星   _____
8 離……更遠   _____
9 岩石構成的；多岩石的 _____
10 環；環狀物   _____
11 塵埃；灰塵   _____
12 小行星帶   _____

20 The Sun and Other Stars

A Listen to the passage and fill in the blanks. 🎧56

Our solar system has many _____ objects other than planets _____ the sun. Two types of these objects are asteroids and _____.

_____ are small, rocky objects that orbit the sun. Many are in the asteroid belt _____ Mars and Jupiter.

Comets are balls that are _____ of ice, rock, and dirt. They orbit the sun, too. Sometimes, when they get near the sun, some of their ice _____ _____ gas. This gives comets _____ that are millions of kilometers long.

What other _____ can you see in the sky? In the night sky, we can see _____ _____ stars. They are all different sizes, ages, and colors. Some groups of stars _____ to form shapes in the night sky. We call these groups of stars _____. The Big _____ and the Little Dipper are two well-known constellations. There are also many _____ in the universe. Galaxies contain _____ _____ stars. Our solar system is on the _____ ____ the Milky Way Galaxy.

B Write the meaning of each word or phrase from Word List in English.

1 天體 _____
2 除了 _____
3 彗星 _____
4 混合物 _____
5 尾巴；尾狀物 _____
6 看起來像 _____
7 星座 _____
8 北斗七星 _____
9 小北斗星 _____
10 星系 _____
11 宇宙 _____
12 包含 _____
13 在……邊緣 _____
14 銀河系 _____

21 What Is Matter?

A Listen to the passage and fill in the blanks. 🎧 57

Everything in the _____ is made of matter. What is _____? Matter is anything that takes _____ space and has mass. All gases, _____, and solids are made of matter.

Matter can be described by its _____. You can tell many kinds of matter apart by _____ their color, size, shape, volume, and mass.

All matter is made of various _____. Elements are the basic _____ that make up all the matter in the universe. There are more than _____ different elements. Some common elements are hydrogen, oxygen, _____, and helium.

Elements can join together to form _____. A compound is a substance that is _____ by the chemical _____ of two or more elements. For example, water is a _____ made up of two elements: _____ and oxygen.

All elements are made of _____. An atom is the smallest _____ of matter. When two or more atoms join together, a _____ is created.

B Write the meaning of each word or phrase from Word List in English.

1	物質	_____	9	氧	_____
2	佔據	_____	10	氮	_____
3	描述	_____	11	氦	_____
4	特性	_____	12	化合物	_____
5	分辨……	_____	13	結合	_____
6	元素	_____	14	原子	_____
7	物質	_____	15	粒子	_____
8	氫	_____	16	分子	_____

22 Changes in Matter

Listen to the passage and fill in the blanks. 🎧 58

Matter often _____ many changes. There are two kinds of changes: _____ changes and chemical changes.

A physical change is a change that does not make a new _____. There are many ways matter can change _____. Matter can change _____. For example, you can find water in its _____ state, liquid state, or _____ state. It _____ different in each state, but it is still the same kind of matter. Making a _____ is another example of a physical change. If you _____ salt into water and stir it, it will _____. You cannot see the salt anymore, but the salt is _____ there.

Matter can also undergo _____ changes. Chemical changes _____ the forming of a new compound. For instance, hydrogen and oxygen are usually two _____ gases. However, if you _____ two hydrogen atoms with one oxygen atom, you get water. This is a chemical _____.

B **Write the meaning of each word or phrase from Word List in English.**

1 物理變化 _____
2 化學變化 _____
3 物理地 _____
4 形態 _____
5 固態 _____
6 液態 _____
7 氣態 _____

8 溶液；溶劑 _____
9 倒；灌 _____
10 攪動；攪拌 _____
11 溶解 _____
12 包含；牽涉 _____
13 不同的 _____
14 結合 _____

23 Taking Care of Our Bodies

A Listen to the passage and fill in the blanks. 🎧59

We sometimes _____ _____. We may catch a cold, the _____, or some other _____. These illnesses are caused by _____ such as viruses and bacteria.

When we get sick, we usually go to the _____. The doctor may give us a _____ or some medicine. After a few days, we typically _____ _____.

However, many _____, like colds and the flu, can spread from one person to another. To stay _____ and strong, we need to practice healthy _____.

First, we need to practice good _____. We should wash our _____ often. We should always wash our hands after using the _____ and before eating.

Also, we need to _____. Exercise _____ our bodies healthy and strong. It also helps our bodies _____ disease.

Eating a _____ diet is also very important. Healthy foods give our _____ energy to work. Unhealthy foods like _____ _____ can make you get sick more _____.

B Write the meaning of each word or phrase from Word List in English.

1	生病	_____	10	藥；內服藥	_____
2	感冒	_____	11	逐漸痊癒	_____
3	流行性感冒	_____	12	嗜好；習慣	_____
4	疾病	d	13	衛生	_____
5	疾病	i	14	運動	_____
6	微生物；病菌	_____	15	均衡的	_____
7	病毒	_____	16	飲食	_____
8	細菌	_____	17	不健康的	_____
9	注射	_____	18	垃圾食物	_____

24 The Six Nutrients

A Listen to the passage and fill in the blanks.

Your body's systems need nutrients to _____ properly. Nutrients are _____ in food that your body _____ to grow and to stay healthy.

There are six kinds of _____. They are carbohydrates, _____, fats, vitamins, minerals, and water. Each nutrient helps the body in a _____ way.

_____ are main source of energy for your body. There are two kinds of carbohydrates: sugars and _____. Foods with starches include rice, _____, and bread. Fruits such as apples and oranges are made of _____.

Proteins are part of every _____ _____. The body needs many proteins to grow and to _____ body cells. Meat, fish, milk, eggs, and _____ products contain proteins.

_____ help your body use other nutrients and _____ energy. But they are needed only in small _____. Fats are found in meats, butter, _____, and oils.

_____ protect you from illnesses. _____ help your blood, muscles, and _____ system.

Water helps your body remove _____. It also keeps your body temperature _____. You could not live for _____ a week without water.

B Write the meaning of each word or phrase from Word List in English.

1	營養物	_____	8	礦物質	_____
2	運作	_____	9	澱粉	_____
3	恰當地;正確地	_____	10	恢復;修補	_____
4	碳水化合物	_____	11	乳製品	_____
5	脂肪;脂質	_____	12	移動;搬移	_____
6	蛋白質	_____	13	廢物	_____
7	維生素;維他命	_____	14	正常的;標準的	_____

🎧 61

A Listen to the passage and fill in the blanks.

Sometimes, we divide _____ numbers into equal parts. We can

_____ these numbers as fractions. For example, if something is divided

into two _____ _____, we can describe one part as $\frac{1}{2}$. _____ is

written in words as one half. If something is divided into _____ equal parts,

each part is ____. $\frac{1}{3}$ is written in _____ as one third.

A _____ has a top number and a bottom number. The top number is the

_____. And the bottom number is the _____. The

denominator _____ how many equal parts there are in the whole. The

numerator represents how many equal parts are being _____.

A _____ number is a combination of a whole number and a fraction. $1\frac{1}{2}$,

_____, and $3\frac{4}{5}$ are mixed numbers.

There are also _____ fractions. These fractions have equal _____

but use different numbers. $\frac{1}{2}$ and _____ are equivalent fractions. So are $\frac{2}{3}$ and

_____.

A fraction that has a numerator of 1, such as _____ and $\frac{1}{3}$, is called a _____

fraction.

B Write the meaning of each word or phrase from Word List in English.

1 整數 _____

2 等分；均分 _____

3 分數 _____

4 分子 _____

5 分母 _____

6 表示 _____

7 帶分數 _____

8 相等的；等值的 _____

9 等值分數 _____

10 單位分數 _____

26 Understanding Fractions

Listen to the passage and fill in the blanks. 🎧 62

1. Here is a _____. Write how many _____ _____ there are. And write the fraction that _____ the shaded part.

   Solution: There are six equal parts. _____ (three sixths) of the whole is _____.

2. Compare $\frac{1}{4}$ and $\frac{2}{4}$. Which one is _____?

   Solution: $\frac{2}{4}$ is greater than _____. When two fractions have the same _____, the one with the greater numerator is the greater fraction.

3. Compare $\frac{1}{4}$ and _____. Which one is greater?

   Solution: _____ is greater than $\frac{1}{8}$. When you _____ or add two fractions with different denominators, you need to make the _____ the same. $\frac{1}{4}$ and $\frac{2}{8}$ are _____ fractions. $\frac{1}{4} =$ _____. So, $\frac{2}{8} > \frac{1}{8}$.

4. Mom cuts an apple into different _____. She gives _____ of the apple to Cindy. And she gives _____ of the apple to Jane. Who has the _____ piece of the apple?

   Solution: $\frac{1}{2}$ is greater _____ $\frac{1}{4}$. ($\frac{1}{2} = \frac{2}{4}$. So, $\frac{2}{4} > \frac{1}{4}$.) So, Jane has the bigger _____ _____ the apple.

5. David orders a pizza and _____ it into 12 slices. David _____ $\frac{1}{3}$ of the pizza. And Steve takes $\frac{1}{4}$ of the _____. How much of the pizza do they take _____?

   Solution: $\frac{1}{3} =$ _____. And $\frac{1}{4} = \frac{3}{12}$. So, $\frac{4}{12} + \frac{3}{12} = \frac{7}{12}$. Together, they take _____ of the pizza.

Write the meaning of each word or phrase from Word List in English.

1 陳述;指定 _____	4 點菜;訂購 _____
2 色彩較暗的 _____	5 切;把……切成薄片 _____
3 比較 _____	6 拿;取 _____

27 Understanding Decimals

A Listen to the passage and fill in the blanks. 🎧 63

You can write the fraction _____ as the _____ 0.1. The period to the left of the 1 is called a _____ _____.

A decimal is a number with one or more _____ to the right of the decimal point. The first place to the right of the decimal point is the _____ place. The second place to the right of the decimal point is the _____ place. The fraction $\frac{1}{100}$ can also be written as the decimal _____. The third place to the right of the decimal point is the _____ place. The fraction _____ can also be written as the decimal _____. You can say $\frac{1}{1000}$ is _____ to 0.001.

Place	Ones		Tenths	Hundredths	Thousandths
Value	0	.	1		
	0	.	0	1	
	0	.	0	0	1

You can write the mixed number _____ as the decimal _____. The mixed number _____ is _____ as a decimal.

Place	Ones		Tenths	Hundredths
Value	1	.	2	
	2	.	1	5

As you read _____, you can change a decimal to an equivalent fraction and a fraction to an _____ _____. Let's _____ changing decimals to equivalent fractions. And, for _____ fraction, _____ the equivalent decimal.

1. 0.4 = _____

2. $\frac{4}{100}$ = _____

3. 0.78 = _____

4. $1\frac{30}{100}$ = _____

B Write the meaning of each word or phrase from Word List in English.

1 小數；小數的 _____

2 小數點 _____

3 數字 _____

4 十分位 _____

5 百分位 _____

6 千分位 _____

7 與……相等的 _____

8 等值小數 _____

28 Reading and Writing Fractions and Decimals

A Listen to the passage and fill in the blanks. 🎧 64

It can sometimes look _____ to read or write a fraction or decimal. But it is _____ really easy.

For fractions, the _____ way is to read the numerator as a _____ number and the denominator as an _____ number. So, _____ = one fourth, _____ = four ninths, and _____ = seven fifteenths.

But there are other _____ to read fractions, too. You could say the fraction $\frac{3}{4}$ is three _____, three out of four, or three _____ by four. So the fraction _____ is two thirds, two _____ _____ three, or two divided by three.

Reading decimals is much _____. Just say each number _____. For example, _____ is two point one. _____ is three point one four. If there is a _____ in front of the decimal point, you must say that, too. So _____ is zero point one.

You can also read some _____ as fractions. For instance, _____ is zero point five or one half. _____ is zero point three three or one third.

B Write the meaning of each word or phrase from Word List in English.

1 令人困惑的 _____
2 基數 _____
3 序數 _____
4 從……裡 _____
5 分別地;逐個地 _____
6 零 _____

29 Norse Mythology

Norse _____ tells stories from Scandinavian countries in Northwest Europe. Today, _____ includes Norway, Sweden, Finland, and Denmark.

A long time ago, many _____ lived in Scandinavia. The Vikings were also called _____. Like the _____ Greeks and Romans, the Vikings had their own myths and _____. Today, we call these stories _____ mythology.

In Norse mythology, there were many gods and _____. Odin was the _____ god. He always had two _____, Thought and Memory. Thor, son of Odin, was the god of _____. When he _____ his mighty hammer, _____ struck, and rain fell onto the earth. Loki was the _____ god. _____ wife Frigg and Thor's wife Freya were two important goddesses. And there were many other _____ and goddesses, too.

The Norse gods all lived in a land called _____. They constantly _____ monsters such as frost _____ and trolls. The Vikings believed that a giant "world tree" called _____ held up the universe. One day, the tree would _____ and bring down the world, _____ a great battle between the gods and giants. Eventually, the _____ would win this battle at Ragnarök and the world would be _____. This was _____ _____ of the world in Norse mythology.

Ⓑ Write the meaning of each word or phrase from Word List in English.

1	古斯堪地那維亞的	_____	9	雷
2	神話	_____	10	擺動
3	維京人	_____	11	巨大的
4	古斯堪地那維亞人	_____	12	鐵鎚
5	古代的	_____	13	雷電
6	傳說；傳奇故事	_____	14	（神話中的）惡作劇精靈；騙子
7	主神	_____		
8	渡鴉	_____	15	戰鬥；戰役

30 Loki the Trickster

A Listen to the passage and fill in the blanks.

🎧 66

Loki was the _____ in Norse mythology. He was the father of Fenrir, the great _____, and of Hel, the goddess of the _____. He often caused many _____ for the gods, especially Thor. But he could help _____, too.

One day, the frost giant Thrym _____ Thor's great hammer. Thrym said he would _____ the hammer if he could _____ Thor's wife Freya. Freya _____, so Loki had an idea. He told Thor to agree to Thrym's _____. But Freya would not really _____ _____. Instead, they would play a _____ on the giant.

Loki dressed up as Freya's _____. And Thor _____ _____ as Freya. Together, they _____ to the giants' land. There, Loki told the giants that Freya was _____ _____ marry Thrym. But it was really Thor in _____. At the _____ party, Thor ate and drank very much. Loki explained, "Freya is _____ to get married. So she is hungry." Thrym wanted to _____ Freya. He lifted the _____ and saw Thor's red eyes. Loki explained, "Freya is so excited that she hasn't _____ for eight days. So her eyes are red."

During the _____, Thrym gave "Freya" the hammer. Thor quickly _____ it and killed all of the giants.

B Write the meaning of each word or phrase from Word List in English.

1 歸還 _____
2 娶；和……結婚 _____
3 拒絕 _____
4 建議；提議 _____
5 結婚 _____
6 捉弄……；對……惡作劇 _____
7 裝扮 _____

8 僕人 _____
9 偽裝；假扮 _____
10 婚禮 _____
11 舉起；抬起 _____
12 面紗；面罩 _____
13 典禮；儀式 _____
14 抓住 _____

31 What Kind of Sentence Is It?

A Listen to the passage and fill in the blanks. 🎧 67

When we speak, we use four different kinds of _____. They are
declarative, interrogative, _____, and exclamatory sentences.
A _____ sentence makes a statement about something. So, it is also
called a _____. We use a _____ to end a declarative sentence:

‣ I like _____.

‣ _____ Johnson lives in the city.

‣ There are three _____ in the pencil case.

We use _____ sentences to ask questions. An interrogative sentence
is also called a _____. These sentences _____ _____ a question mark:

‣ What _____ is it?

‣ Where are you _____?

‣ What will I be when I _____ _____?

An imperative sentence or a _____ gives orders or directions. In an
imperative sentence, the _____ of the sentence is "you." But you do not
_____ "you." These sentences end with a period or an _____ point:

‣ Open the _____.

‣ Be _____!

‣ Go home _____ _____.

We use _____ sentences or exclamations when we are _____
or excited about something. _____ sentences end with an exclamation point:

‣ That's _____! ‣ I can't _____ it! ‣ _____!

B Write the meaning of each word or phrase from Word List in English.

1 直述句 _____

2 陳述句；陳述 _____

3 疑問句 _____

4 問句；問題 _____

5 祈使句 _____

6 命令 _____

7 感嘆句 _____

8 驚嘆；感嘆；感嘆句 _____

9 以……結束 _____

10 問號 _____

11 主詞 _____

12 驚嘆號 _____

13 感到驚訝 _____

14 驚人的；令人吃驚的 _____

A Listen to the passage and fill in the blanks. 🎧 68

There are many kinds of _____ marks in English. We use them in different _____.

We _____ use a punctuation mark at the end of a sentence. Most sentences end with a _____ (.). However, if you are _____ a question, use a question mark (?) at the end. If you are making an _____, use an exclamation point (!) _____ _____ _____.

But we also use punctuation _____ in the middle of a sentence. One _____ punctuation mark is a comma (,). A comma is like a _____ in the middle of a sentence. The following sentences need _____:

▸ I like apples, oranges, and _____.

▸ Eric is a student, but John is a _____.

Use a colon (:) to _____ things or add explanations:

▸ You can use a colon in _____ ways: to make lists or to give _____.

Use a _____ (—) to show a pause in a sentence:

▸ Jay—my brother—is going to do his _____ right now.

And use _____ (" ") to show that a person is speaking:

▸ He said, "_____ open the door."

There are also other punctuation marks, such as a semicolon (;), _____ (-), and slash (/).

B Write the meaning of each word or phrase from Word List in English.

1	標點符號	_____	5	列舉	_____
2	情況	_____	6	破折號	_____
3	逗號	_____	7	引號	_____
4	暫停	_____	8	連字號	_____

33 Appreciating Artwork

A Listen to the passage and fill in the blanks. 🎧 69

Museums and art ＿＿＿＿＿ exhibit all kinds of paintings. In many ＿＿＿＿＿ and art galleries, you can find great ＿＿＿＿＿ of art called masterpieces.

What makes a ＿＿＿＿＿? There are many ＿＿＿＿＿ of painting. Many paintings have ＿＿＿＿＿ between light and shadows and ＿＿＿＿＿ colors and dark colors. Lines, shapes, and ＿＿＿ ＿＿＿＿＿ ＿＿＿ space are very important, too. Realistic artists and ＿＿＿＿＿ artists use lines, shapes, and space differently.

Many ＿＿＿＿＿ also have a foreground, background, and middle ground. The ＿＿＿＿＿ is the objects that are ＿＿＿＿＿ to you. In the foreground, things are larger and more ＿＿＿＿＿ colored than anything else in the painting. The ＿＿＿＿＿ is the objects that are ＿＿＿＿＿ from you. They ＿＿＿＿＿ smaller. The ＿＿＿＿＿ ground is those ＿＿＿＿＿ that are between the foreground and the background. This ＿＿＿＿＿ makes paintings look more realistic.

All these different elements ＿＿＿＿＿ ＿＿＿＿＿ in every painting. ＿＿＿＿＿ design the right ＿＿＿＿＿ ＿＿＿ these elements in their works and make great works.

B Write the meaning of each word or phrase from Word List in English.

1	博物館 ＿＿＿＿＿	8	現實主義的 ＿＿＿＿＿
2	美術館；畫廊 ＿＿＿＿＿	9	抽象主義的 ＿＿＿＿＿
3	陳列；展覽 ＿＿＿＿＿	10	前景 ＿＿＿＿＿
4	名作；名著 ＿＿＿＿＿	11	背景 ＿＿＿＿＿
5	成分；要素 ＿＿＿＿＿	12	（距離、時間上）最遠的 ＿＿＿＿＿
6	對比；對照 ＿＿＿＿＿	13	似乎；看來好像 ＿＿＿＿＿
7	空間感 ＿＿＿＿＿	14	透視畫法 ＿＿＿＿＿

A Listen to the passage and fill in the blanks. 🎧 70

When _____ create art, they design their work by _____ lines, shapes, and colors. Symmetry and balance are two important _____ using lines and shapes.

The ancient _____ created many beautiful paintings, buildings, and _____. Their art deeply _____ other artists in later years. The ancient Greeks _____ balance and _____ to be the most important qualities of art. Ancient Greek buildings are _____ balanced and _____. Symmetry and balance make something a _____ work of art. The _____ is the most famous symmetric building.

Color is another _____ element of design. There are three _____ colors: red, yellow, and blue. By mixing two primary colors together, we can make the three _____ colors. They are orange, green, and _____. Complementary colors are found _____ one another on the color _____. Red and green are _____ colors that go together. So are blue and _____ and yellow and purple.

B Write the meaning of each word or phrase from Word List in English.

1	對稱	_____	9	對稱的	_____ al
2	平衡；均衡	_____	10	對稱的	_____ c
3	特徵；特色	_____	11	基本的；必要的	_____
4	雕刻品；雕像	_____	12	原色	_____
5	影響	_____	13	二次色	_____
6	往後幾年裡	_____	14	在……的對面	_____
7	認為	_____	15	色環；色輪	_____
8	比例	_____	16	互補色	_____

35 Elements of Music

A Listen to the passage and fill in the blanks.

When composers _____ music _____, they use special _____ called notes. The _____ tell us the _____ and the length of musical sounds. The composers also tell us the _____—how high or low the notes should be—by _____ the notes high or low on a staff.

When you sing or play these notes _____ _____ _____, you are singing or playing a musical _____. There are seven main notes on a _____ scale: A, B, C, D, E, F, and G. The notes on a musical scale all have a _____ pitch. There are a _____ scale of notes and a _____ scale of notes.

There are also _____ and flat notes. A sharp note _____ the pitch of a note by half a step. A _____ note decreases the pitch of a note by _____ a step.

At the beginning of a _____, there is a special mark called a _____ _____, or a G clef. The treble clef _____ where the G note on the staff is.

B Write the meaning of each word or phrase from Word List in English.

1　作曲者；作曲家　_____
2　音符　_____
3　音高　_____
4　五線譜　_____
5　接連地；連續不斷地 _____
6　音階　_____
7　大調音階　_____
8　小調音階　_____
9　升記號　_____
10　降記號　_____
11　高音譜號　_____
12　G 譜號　_____

36 Musical Instructions

A Listen to the passage and fill in the blanks. 🎧72

Composers _____ sounds by placing musical notes on a staff. Sometimes they give more _____ instructions.

Two common _____ are legato and staccato. When musicians play _____, they should play the musical notes _____ without breaks. But _____ should be played in the _____ way. When _____ play staccato, they should play each note by making a short, _____ sound.

Also, the _____ of the music are important. This _____ _____ how loud or soft the music should be. The instructions are found in these _____: p, pp, mp, f, ff, and mf.

p means _____. This means a musician should play _____. pp means _____, which is "very softly." And mp means _____ piano, which is "_____ softly."

Sometimes musicians should play _____. f means _____. This _____ a musician should play loudly. ff means _____, which is "very loudly." And mf means mezzo forte, _____ is "moderately loudly."

_____ instruction is Da Capo al Fine. Da Capo means "from the _____." Al Fine means "to _____ _____." Da Capo al Fine instructs the musician to _____ from the beginning _____ _____ the word Fine.

B Write the meaning of each word or phrase from Word List in English.

1 表現；描述 _____
2 明確的；詳盡的 _____
3 指示；說明 _____
4 連奏；連奏地 _____
5 斷奏；斷奏地 _____
6 以相反的方式 _____
7 適度地；中等地 _____
8 大聲地 _____
9 重複 _____
10 一直到 _____

MEMO

Answer Key

Lesson 1 Previewing P. 6

Part 1

1. YES   2. YES   3. YES

4. The sequential format of the passage tells me that the role of clowns has changed over time.

Part 2

The passage is about clowns and how they have changed over time.

Part 3

1. Previewing the title helped me know that the passage is about more than just what clowns do now.
2. Previewing the photograph helped me think of what I already know about clowns, such as their costumes and jobs.
3. Previewing the passage helped me to better understand what the text is about.

Comprehension Review

1. D   2. C   3. B   4. C   5. D   6. A

Word Power

1. amuse   2. unique   3. distract   4. perform

Lesson 2 Cause and Effect—Plot
P. 10

Part 1

1. They start on the bike ride at 7 A.M.
2. They don't stop for lunch until noon.
3. They have a picnic under an oak tree.
4. There is a storm coming, and the bikers need to get away from it.

Part 2

1. The sky becomes very dark.
2. The trees are bending in the wind.

Part 3

1. Maria screams, "It's a tornado!"
2. The narrator is terrified.
3. Maria's mother yells at them to get in the car.
4. They are safe in the storm cellar.

Comprehension Review

1. B   2. D   3. A   4. C   5. B   6. C

Word Power

1. colossal   2. funnel   3. roaring   4. avoid

Lesson 3 Headings to Determine Main Ideas P. 14

Part 1

Jeans	The first jeans were invented for gold miners, who needed strong pockets.

Part 2

Jeans	Levi Strauss invented them for gold miners in 1873.
Raincoats	Charles Macintosh made the first waterproof cloth.
Shoes	Today, shoe pieces are mainly cut and put together on machines.

Part 3

1. The copper rivets make the pockets strong.
2. Jeans were invented in 1873.
3. Charles Macintosh made the first waterproof cloth.
4. The person who makes shoes is called a *cobbler*.

Comprehension Review

1. A   2. C   3. B   4. D   5. C   6. A

Word Power

1. rivet   2. garment   3. waterproof   4. cobbler

2

Lesson 4 Main Idea P. 18

Part 1

The eye is an incredible structure that works with the brain to help people see.

Part 2

Main Idea
The eye is an amazing structure that allows people to see.

	Supporting Detail
1	Your eyes send messages to your brain.
2	The cornea is like a window that lets light into the eyeball.
3	The iris controls the amount of light that comes through the pupil.
4	The retina sends messages to the brain so you know what you are seeing.

Comprehension Review

1. B   2. C   3. A   4. D   5. B   6. A

Word Power

1. coating   2. message   3. control   4. structure

Lesson 5 Compare and Contrast
P. 22

Part 1

Pencils	Both	Pens
• Made of wood • Have erasers	• Can write on paper • Made in a factory	• Use ink • Have caps

Part 2

Similarities: They both tell time.

Differences: Digital timers use computer technology; manual stopwatches do not.

Part 3

Same: Manual stopwatches and digital timers both measure time.

Different: anual stopwatches can only measure down to 0.50 of a second, but digital timers can measure down to 0.001.

Comprehension Review

1. D   2. C   3. A   4. C   5. B   6. D

Word Power

1. accurate   2. manual   3. athlete   4. digital

Lesson 6 Topic to Predict P. 26

Part 1

I think I will learn about different animals that live at the zoo.

Part 2

I think the rest of the passage will be about the history of zoos.

Part 3

Zoos have changed over time. Most zoos no longer keep animals in cages. Most of the animals in zoos have never lived in the wild. A zoo can also help endangered animals. It can breed species that no longer exist in the wild and sometimes can even reintroduce them to their natural habitats.

Comprehension Review

1. C   2. D   3. A   4. C   5. B   6. D

Word Power

1. modern   2. endangered   3. captive   4. rare

Lesson 7 Character P. 30

Part 1

I imagined Mrs. Gerson as an older woman because of how the author said she ambled out onto the field. I pictured her with short white hair and wrinkles on her face.

Part 2

Mrs. Gerson is a lot of fun. I think she probably likes to try new things even if she doesn't know what to expect, so she is adventurous. She is outgoing and brave because she is not afraid to look silly.

Part 3

Trait: adventurous

How it is shown in the passage:

The author shows that Mrs. Gerson is adventurous when she marches to home plate and picks up the bat. She doesn't know how to hold it properly, so she swings it wildly.

She also shows her adventurous side when she tells the boys that they can have their ball back if they let her hit a home run.

Mrs. Gerson is not afraid to try hitting a home run even though it sounds like she has never done it before. She even raises her arms in victory when she crosses home plate.

Comprehension Review

1. D   2. B   3. C   4. A   5. C   6. D

Word Power

1. approach   2. determined

3. amble   4. pretend

Lesson 8 Topic Sentences to Determine Main Ideas P. 34

Part 1

Earth's spinning causes a cycle of changing seasons.

Part 2

T	Earth is a planet.
1	Earth is a planet.
2	Earth is the third planet from the sun.
3	Earth is the only planet known to have life on it.

Part 3

1. B   2. A   3. B

Comprehension Review

1. A   2. C   3. B   4. D   5. A   6. B

Word Power

1. orbit   2. axis   3. tilt   4. cycle

Lesson 9 Prior Knowledge P. 38

Part 1

2. The passage will be about firefighters.

3. The passage will tell about the work of firefighters.

Part 2

2. What do firefighters do when they are not fighting a fire?

3. What type of equipment do firefighters use?

Part 3

1. When they are not fighting fires, firefighters go to schools to help educate people, they practice putting out fires, and they take care of their equipment.

2. Firefighters use fire trucks, hoses, and nozzles.

Comprehension Review

1. C   2. B   3. D   4. A   5. D   6. B

Word Power

1. equipment   2. emergency

3. safety   4. chore

Lesson 10 Sequential Order P. 42

Part 1

Next	Then

Part 2

1. Keep track of your income and expenses by writing down what you earn and spend.

2. Plan ahead and decide what you need to save money for.

3. Make a list of what you will earn.

4. Make a list of what you will spend.

5. Add up your total income and subtract the total expenses.

Part 3

It is important to make a budget, and it takes only a few steps. The first step is tracking how much you make, or your incomes. You should also track how much you spend, or your expense. You can do this by writing both down for a few weeks. Next, think about what you will need money for and how you will earn it. Then, make a list of what you will earn and what you'll spend in the futrue. Finally, do the math. Subtract your expenses from your income, and you'll know how much of your budget you can save.

Comprehension Review

1. A   2. D   3. B   4. A   5. A   6. C

Word Power

1. allowance   2. income

3. expense   4. subtract

Lesson 11 Meaning Clues to Predict
P. 46

Part 1

1. The passage will be about matter.

2. Judging from the photos, ice is a solid.

3. The passage will describe solids, liquids, and gases.

Part 2

YES	My predictions were correct because the passage is about matter and ice is a solid. Also, the passage explains about solids, liquids, and gases.
Title and **Photo**	The title gave me hints, and the photos provided visual images.

Part 3

Making predictions helps me review what I know about the topic and makes me curious to learn more.

Comprehension Review

1. B   2. A   3. C   4. D   5. A   6. B

Word Power

1. evaporate   2. state   3. substance   4. melt

Lesson 12 Problem and Solution— Plot P. 50

Part 1

1. She never told the teacher or her parents.

2. No, because she didn't want to be a bully.

3. Tia told her to stop picking on her friend.

Part 2

The setting is a school.

Part 3

Problem: A new girl picked on Tia's friend.

Solution: Tia told the new girl to stop picking on her friend.

Comprehension Review

1. C   2. D   3. A   4. B   5. A   6. D

Word Power

1. ashamed   2. bully   3. forgive   4. tease

Lesson 13 Captions to Determine Main Ideas P. 54

Part 1

The roles of family members have changed over time.

Part 2

Families today spend more time having fun together than families in the past did.

Part 3

Left: In the past, all members of the family worked to make their clothes.

Right: Today, people work hard but also have more free time to spend with their families.

Comprehension Review

1. B   2. C   3. A   4. B   5. D   6. C

Word Power

1. chore   2. provide   3. invention   4. repair

Lesson 14 Graphic Features P. 58

Part 1
I learned that the water in lakes and oceans evaporates.

Part 2
1. The diagram shows the water cycles.
2. The water in lakes and oceans evaporates.
3. Rivers carry water from lakes to the ocean.
4. Precipitation is rain.

Part 3
The main idea is to provide information about desert.

Comprehension Review
1. A   2. D   3. B   4. C   5. A   6. D

Word Power
1. evaporation   2. form
3. precipitation   4. extreme

Lesson 15 Chronological Order P. 62

Part 1
| history books | directions | recipes |

Part 2
1984	Sally Ride flew with the Challenger crew.
1982	She was named to the crew of the seventh space shuttle flight.
1951	Sally Ride was born in Los Angeles, California.

Part 3
1. The year Sally Ride went to college.
2. The year Sally Ride read the ad by NASA.

Comprehension Review
1. A   2. C   3. B   4. A   5. C   6. D

Word Power
1. crew   2. encourage
3. respect   4. exploration

Lesson 16 Structure to Predict P. 66

Part 1
I predict I will be reading about some handmade African art.

Part 2
In this passage, I will learn about African textiles and jewelry.

Part 3
This section will be about African art made from textiles.

Part 4
This section will describe jewelry worn in Africa.

Comprehension Review
1. B   2. A   3. D   4. C   5. B   6. A

Word Power
1. material   2. weave   3. texture   4. fabric

Lesson 17 Author's Purpose P. 70

Part 1
2. Women won the right to vote in 1920.
3. Eleanor Roosevelt wanted all people to have the same rights.
4. Marian Anderson was a well-known singer during the 1930s.

Part 2
I don't think the author of this passage was trying to entertain me. I didn't find the passage funny or delightful. I think the author was trying to teach me something about Eleanor Roosevelt and how she was a champion for change. I learned that she asked politicians to work for civil rights when she was First Lady.

Part 3
1. Yes
2. The author wants readers to support the rights of all people, regardless of race or gender.
3. Yes

Comprehension Review

1. C 2. A 3. B 4. D 5. C 6. B

Word Power

1. right 2. equal 3. goal 4. civil rights

Lesson 18 Chapter Titles to Determine Main Ideas

P. 74

Part 1

This passage will be about a Hispanic American man named Roberto Clemente.

Part 2

2. Roberto was on two teams that won the World Series.

3. He was the Most Valuable Player in the 1971 World Series.

4. He was voted into the Baseball Hall of Fame.

Part 3

Roberto Clemente was a great man because he achieved many things during his life and dedicated his time and money to helping others.

Comprehension Review

1. C 2. B 3. A 4. D 5. C 6. B

Word Power

1. champion 2. donate 3. supplies 4. deliver

Lesson 19 Logical Order P. 78

Part 1

I follow a set of directions whenever I help in the kitchen. Last week, we made cookies. I looked at the ingredients needed and then followed the numbered steps in the recipe. I followed the directions exactly, so the cookies tasted good when they were done.

Part 2

1. I need one tube of wood glue.

2. Step 4 says to push the perch into the hole on the front of the birdhouse.

3. I should hang my birdhouse in a secluded spot in a tree or under the eaves of the roof.

4. I need 2 side pieces and 2 front and end pieces.

Part 3

1. B 2. D 3. A 4. D 5. C

Comprehension Review

1. C 2. B 3. D 4. B 5. A 6. D

Word Power

1. eave 2. perch 3. secluded 4. kit

Lesson 20 Fact and Opinion P. 82

Part 1

1. F 2. F 3. T

Part 2

| great | pretty | fine | excellent |

Part 3

Fact
2. The leaves of the sugar maple turn a rich yellow, orange, or deep red in the fall.
3. The bark of the tree is flaky and gray.
4. The sugar maple grows 75–100 feet tall.

Opinion
2. The wood of the maple makes pretty furniture and cabinets.
3. The leaves look like someone painted them with a giant brush.
4. If you are looking for an excellent tree to plant in your yard, choose the sugar maple.

Comprehension Review

1. A 2. C 3. D 4. B 5. A 6. D

Word Power

1. sap 2. rich 3. bare 4. syrup

Lesson 21 Monitoring Reading Strategies P. 86

Part 1

I was thinking that the ant was not being very kind to the chrysalis and probably thought it was better than the chrysalis.

Part 2

1. Yes   2. Yes   3. Yes   4. Yes   5. Yes   6. Yes

Part 3

1. chrysalis	4. remained
2. metamorphosis	5. shaded
3. pitiful	6. deceiving

Comprehension Review

1. D   2. C   3. B   4. A   5. C   6. B

Word Power

1. metamorphosis   2. imprisoned
3. boast   4. attract

Lesson 22 Purpose for Reading P. 90

Part 1

When previewing the text, I noticed that there is a date and a time listed. I noticed the note at the bottom about the snack. There is a picture of a girl looking at a cat in a tree, which I think is from the story Alice in Wonderland.

Part 2

I read for entertainment, to learn what someone thinks about something, and to get information.

Part 3

1. a thank you note from a friend
   Because I like when my friend writes to me.
2. a restaurant menu
   Because it doesn't have a lot of words.

Comprehension Review

1. A   2. D   3. B   4. C   5. A   6. D

Word Power

1. version   2. direct   3. adventure   4. fantasy

Lesson 23 Cause and Effect P. 94

Part 1

2.	**Cause:** Your stomach is empty.
	Effect: Your stomach contracts.
3.	**Cause:** You don't eat.
	Effect: Your stomach begins to contract more frequently.
4.	**Cause:** You are happy.
	Effect: The food you eat is quickly digested.

Part 2

2. When your stomach is empty, it contracts as a result.
3. If you are happy, the food you eat is quickly digested.

Part 3

Food will sit in your stomach.
1. You are sad.
2. You are angry.

Comprehension Review

1. B   2. A   3. D   4. C   5. B   6. C

Word Power

1. contract   2. digest   3. glucose   4. wonder

Lesson 24 Summary Sentences P. 98

Part 1

A summary sentence is a single sentence from a passage that tells what the text is mostly about.

Part 2

To make a real difference, something big had to happen outside of the courtroom.

Part 3

Many people fought against segregation in many different ways.

Comprehension Review

1. C   2. B   3. A   4. C   5. D   6. A

Word Power

1. protest   2. segregation
3. boycott   4. association

Lesson 25 Retelling P. 102

Part 1

The Chesapeake Bay is located in the eastern United States. It is not only a vacation spot, but also home to some of the most famous coastal wetlands.

Part 2

A wetland has many features, including shallow water and plants and animals live both above and below the water.

Part 3

Wetlands are home to many plants and animal. Animals and other creatures use the decaying material from plants and trees for food.

Comprehension Review

1. D   2. A   3. B   4. B   5. D   6. B

Word Power

1. bay   2. shallow   3. habitat   4. locate

Lesson 26 Selecting Reading Material P. 106

Part 1

1. This is probably a nonfiction book.
2. I am very interested in this kind of book because it seems interesting. I don't know much about Hatshepsut and would like to learn more.

Part 2

1. I like to read action books for fun.
2. J. K. Rowling is my favorite author.
3. To learn about a topic, I like to read books that have lots of photographs and diagrams.
4. Books that persuade me about a topic are realistic fiction books.

Part 3

One of the best books I have read recently is *Harry Potter and the Order of the Phoenix*. It has a lot of action; it keeps you thinking, and it's hard to put down. I have also learned a lot about England by reading the book.

Comprehension Review

1. A   2. D   3. C   4. C   5. A   6. C

Word Power

1. decision   2. civilization
3. monument   4. serve

Lesson 27 Typeface P. 110

Part 1

1. This will explain how the census counts people.
2. This will tell how information is gathered.
3. This will explain what the information in the census is used for.

Part 2

1. This section tells how governments count the people who live in their countries.
2. This section tells how the census is conducted.
3. This section tells how census data is used.

Part 3

1. simple letters
2. fancy letters
3. simple letters
4. fancy letters
5. simple letters

Comprehension Review

1. D   2. C   3. A   4. B   5. A   6. B

Word Power

1. data　　2. predict　　3. population　　4. decide

Lesson 28 Proposition and Support

P. 114

Part 1

Summer vacation is too long.

Part 2

The proposed solution to the problem is to have year-round schools.

Part 3

I propose	in this model
instead	I think

Comprehension Review

1. B　　2. C　　3. D　　4. A　　5. C　　6. D

Word Power

1. achievement　　2. traditional

3. propose　　4. model

Lesson 29 Summarizing

P. 118

Part 1

1. Ballerinas and danseurs
2. It's a kind of performance.
3. It began in Italy.
4. Most people start to learn ballet at 3 or 4 years old.
5. They practice because they love ballet.
6. He must practice very hard.

Part 2

Ballet dancers are athletes.

Part 3

　　Ballet dancers are athletes. Ballet may be beautiful, but it is hard work. These early lessons include learning ballet positions. When they are three or four years old. They are taught ballet positions, and when they are about 11 or 12, they have lessons daily. Both boys and girls can be ballet dancers, but they all must work very hard. They must be fit and strong. If they are successful athletes, they can join a ballet company.

Comprehension Review

1. A　　2. D　　3. B　　4. C　　5. B　　6. A

Word Power

1. perform　　2. training　　3. pose　　4. athletic

Lesson 30 Questioning

P. 122

Part 1

2.	**Question:** How did the lion get a bone stuck in his mouth?
	Answer: He got it stuck while he was eating dinner.
3.	**Question:** How did the woodpecker know the lion was in trouble?
	Answer: The woodpecker heard the lion when it was perched in a tree.

Part 2

1. Yes, it's a good idea for the woodpecker to be careful.
2. I didn't think the lion would try to eat the woodpecker because the woodpecker helped him when he was in trouble.

Part 3

2.	**Question:** How did the woodpecker protect itself?
	Answer: It put a large stick in the lion's mouth so it wouldn't get eaten.
3.	**Question:** Can the woodpecker trust the lion?
	Answer: No, the lion doesn't want to repay the favor to the woodpecker.

Comprehension Review

1. D　　2. C　　3. A　　4. D　　5. B　　6. C

Word Power

1. ail　　2. expect　　3. perch　　4. dare

Lesson 1　古之弄臣，今之小丑 P. 5

我們聽到「小丑」這個字，通常會想到馬戲團。然而小丑在加入馬戲團表演前，他們這一行早就已經存在了。

一開始，小丑被稱為「弄臣」。他們活躍於中古世紀的宮廷中，負責逗國王與王室成員開心。弄臣身穿特別的服裝，全身行頭包括滑稽帽和繫著小鈴噹的尖靴。每當他們為國王表演時，靴上的鈴鐺便會隨之晃動，發出悅耳的叮噹聲，替他們的演出增添趣味。弄臣通常與他們所服侍的王室成員非常親近。他們也會陪宮廷的孩子們玩樂、參與王室家族活動。弄臣不僅滑稽，通常也非常聰慧，有些弄臣甚至會為他們服侍的王室成員出主意。

美國早期馬戲團裡的小丑就像是詼諧逗趣的喜劇演員，他們在環狀的舞台上唱歌、跳舞、講笑話。後來馬戲團發展出三個環狀的表演舞台，小丑便開始表演啞劇，也就是不講話，只憑藉肢體動作來演出。

如今，小丑在馬戲團與牛仔競技場上表演。在馬戲團裡，他們帶來歡樂，經常要在緊張刺激的特技表演間串場。有些小丑也會表演逗趣版的特技或雜耍，而且十八般武藝樣樣精通。他們會走鋼索、會在空中表演特技，還會無鞍騎馬。在牛仔競技場上，小丑逗得觀眾哈哈大笑。此外，他們也要負責引開危險動物的注意力，讓其他人藉機將傷者從競技場上救下來。

小丑的表演服裝與化妝方式向來獨一無二，不同類型的小丑必須化不同的妝。大多數的小丑都是「白臉小丑」，他們在整張臉抹上「小丑白」的油彩，然後再以其他顏色畫出眼睛跟嘴巴。小丑的鼻子通常是以特殊的油灰做成。
美國與其他國家都有許多一流的小丑。

Lesson 2　跟龍捲風賽跑 P. 8

如果當時我們知道接下來會發生什麼事情，我們決對不會騎腳踏車外出。可是那天的天氣很好，適合騎遠程，所以 Maria 跟我早上七點鐘就騎著腳踏車出發，直到中午才停下來吃午餐。我們坐在橡樹下野餐。這時候天氣起了變化，我們也開始擔心了。遠方出現一團高聳的烏雲。我們面面相覷，心下明白我們沒有辦法避開那個龍捲風。

不久天氣變得更惡劣，天空烏雲密布，樹木因強風而折腰。突然間，有輛黃色的車停在我們的腳踏車旁。開車的婦人是 Maria 的媽媽，她打開車門，對我們大喊：「上車！」她看起來跟我們一樣，也是一副很害怕的樣子。

我們一上車，天空就開始下起巨大的冰雹。汽車火速駛離，冰雹打在引擎蓋上紛紛彈開。Maria 跟我兩人回過頭看著陰暗的天空，Maria 尖叫：「是龍捲風！」漆黑的漏斗似乎又更接近我們了。我嚇壞了。我們怎麼跑得贏那個凶猛的怪物呢？ Maria 的媽媽回頭看我們一眼說：「奶奶家就快到了，我知道她有個防風窖，我們到那裡躲一躲。」她一路狂飆，猛然地駛入一條狹窄的馬路。不久，車子發出尖銳刺耳的煞車聲，車子停了下來。Maria 的媽媽對我們大吼，要我們馬上進防風窖。我們衝出車門，一路狂奔進了地窖，分秒不差地逃過龍捲風的侵襲。龍捲風的怒吼聲宛如載貨火車般，從地窖上方呼嘯而過。突然間一切都結束了，我們差一點就來不及躲過龍捲風。這絕對是一場我們不想要再比一次的賽跑。

Lesson 3　衣服的歷史 P. 12

你看著你的衣櫃說：「媽，我沒有衣服穿！我們可以去逛街買衣服嗎？」你接下來可能會在服飾店待好幾個小時選衣服，想買穿起來舒服，又能讓你看起來亮眼的衣服。但是衣服到底是怎麼來的？是誰做的？又是怎麼做的？

牛仔褲

如果你跟大多數人一樣，那麼你一定有牛仔褲。Levi Strauss 在 1873 年為採金礦的礦工發明了牛仔褲。現在的牛仔褲看起來跟當時的差不多，口袋上仍有銅鉚釘。Strauss 加上銅鉚釘是為了讓口袋更牢固，好讓礦工們在裡面裝金塊。

雨衣

如果你有雨衣，那你得好好感謝 Charles Macintosh，因為他製作出第一件防水衣。他在兩層布料間塗上一層薄薄的橡膠，布料上特殊的液體能幫助橡膠附著，然後再把這塊布製成雨衣。大家都很愛這個發明！因為就算下雨，也不會被雨淋濕。

鞋子

很多年前，鞋匠只在客人下單後，才會開始製做鞋子。他們會先量顧客腳的尺寸，再選擇適合的鞋版。鞋匠用這個鞋版來裁剪皮革鞋面與鞋底，然後再將裁好的皮革鞋面一片片縫起來。最後，他們用小木釘將鞋面與鞋底釘起來。做一雙鞋通常要花上好幾天的時間。現在製鞋的主要工作都是由機器來完成，以機器裁剪、縫製鞋面與鞋底。有些鞋子是用縫的，有些則是用黏的。如此一來，鞋子的成本更低，大家就買得起更多雙的鞋子。

Lesson 4　視力　P. 16

視覺能讓你看見身邊周遭的世界。你的眼睛會將看到的訊息傳送到大腦，而大腦則告訴你看到了什麼。視覺是我們生活在這個世界上最重要的方式之一。你曾經戴過眼罩嗎？如果你戴過，那麼你就會知道看不到的日子有多麼難過。

眼睛的構造很神奇。眼白的部分叫做鞏膜，它的外層包覆著大部分的眼球。角膜是鞏膜的一部分，無色透明，且包覆眼珠，作用就像是窗戶，能讓光線進入眼球。虹膜與瞳孔位於角膜的後方；虹膜的部分含有色素，而瞳孔則是虹膜中心黑色的部分。虹膜能控制進入瞳孔的光線多寡。光線昏暗時，虹膜會讓瞳孔放大一些，好讓更多的光線進入眼睛；光線明亮時，虹膜則讓瞳孔縮小，只讓少量的光線進入眼睛。

進入眼睛的光線會傳到水晶體，水晶體將影像聚焦在眼球後方的視網膜上，然後視網膜會將接收到的訊息傳送到大腦，而大腦則會告訴你眼中所見的事物是甚麼。

Lesson 5　計時比賽　P. 20

知道誰贏得比賽是很重要的。運動員若贏得比賽，就能獲得獎金。要是能打破世界紀錄，領到的獎金就更多了。

很久以前，人們使用手動碼表計時。不過，這些手動碼表只能精確到 0.50 秒，而現在使用的數位碼表則可精確到 0.001 秒。

1932 年的奧林匹克運動會很特殊，因為那年的奧運首度改採自動電子碼表來計時。不過，那時也只能精確到 0.10 秒。1932 年奧運的 100 公尺賽跑男子組的冠軍以 10.30 秒贏得比賽。可是，第三名的運動員卻跑出 10.40 秒的成績。1/10（0.10）秒在短跑比賽中是很長的時間。現今，起步槍一響，數位碼表也開始同步計時，這樣計時就更準確了。

現在的碼表可以精確測量到 0.001 秒！起跑器上都有擴音器，賽跑選手能聽到從擴音器裡傳來起步槍開槍的聲音。所有的選手都能同時聽到槍響。在聽到槍響後，選手立刻飛奔而去。如果有選手在槍未鳴便先動身，我們稱之為「搶跑」。下一個搶跑的選手就會被取消參賽資格，也就是說選手必須要離場。

2004 年奧運的終點線改採雷射光束。選手抵達終點線「衝破」光束時，也同時結束計時。以雷射光束來替賽跑計時的確是相當準確的方式。

Lesson 6　新舊動物園　P. 24

古代中國的統治者向來喜歡私下收藏動物，不過第一座動物園早在西元前 1500 年就已存在於埃及，那就是哈姬蘇女王的動物園。園中的動物都是獻給女王的貢禮，每當軍隊佔領一地時，就會有人將當地的珍禽野獸做為貢禮進獻給女王。

在現代的動物園成立前，有人會向大眾展覽私下豢養的野生動物，人稱 menagerie，也就是「小動物園」之意。這些小動物園裡的野生動物都是豢養在又髒又小的籠子裡。有鑑於此，這才產生了現代的動物園。現在的動物園是將野生動物養在與其自然棲息地相似的環境裡。但是這樣的改變並不是一蹴可幾。許多年來，世界最大、最現代化的動物園和其他動物園都還是把動物關在籠子裡。即便是現在，也還有動物園會把動物豢養在籠子裡。報紙上依舊可見到反對此舉的文章，反對這種對待動物的方式。

很久以前，成立動物園的目的是讓民眾觀賞從遠地抓來的稀有動物，因為許多人終其一生都不可能有機會去那麼遠的地方。但如今，在動物園裡豢養野生動物卻有其他原因。例如，許多野生動物瀕臨絕種，這表示已經很難在自然棲息地看到這些野生動物。而有些動物已經從野外絕跡,如今只能在某些地方見到他們。動物學家們有時候能成功繁殖這些被圈養的野生動物,他們也試著幫助動物回到他們的自然棲息地。但是動物學家也不是每次都能這麼做,很多時候都是因為土地使用的變更,導致野生動物的自然棲息地消失。

曾有一度,獵人會獵捕野生動物,再轉賣給有需要的動物園。雖然現在還是有人這麼做,不過現在動物園間通常會買賣或交易彼此的動物。所以你在動物園裡看到的動物可能從來沒在野外生活過,他們都是在動物園裡出生,以人工飼養方式養大的。

動物權人士不喜歡看到動物園展示這些野生動物。不過,有些人反倒覺得動物園關懷保護這些動物。他們認為這就是為什麼許多珍禽異獸還能存活到現在原因。

Lesson 7　格爾森奶奶的全壘打　P. 28

事情的開始是這樣的:大麥克擊出一支全壘打,把球打進格爾森奶奶家的前院。等男孩們反應過來時,格爾森奶奶已經手裡拿著棒球,好像拿著一顆臭雞蛋一樣,緩慢地走向棒球場。

「你們這些小鬼!」她說,「我跟你們說過,不可以把球打進我的院子裡!」

「格爾森奶奶,對不起!」尼克說,「可以把球還給我們嗎?」

「可以,我可以把球還給你們,」她接著說,「只要你們讓我打出一支全壘打。」老奶奶堅決地走到本壘板,撿起丟在地上的球棒。

當這些男孩們不知道該如何是好時,格爾森奶奶已經站上本壘板,雙手舉著球棒在頭上揮舞著。凱文只好拿著棒球站到投手丘,盡可能輕柔地將球投向本壘。格爾森奶奶亂揮球棒,不知怎麼地居然打中了球。

「快跑!」男孩們一塊兒大喊。

老奶奶便開始跑向一壘。湯米從本壘板走去把球撿起來,但老奶奶連一壘的一半都還跑不到,所以湯米只好將球高高地投過一壘手的上方。尼克盡可能慢慢地撿起球,而老奶奶正好走到一壘。

「那邊!」麥克指著二壘的方向。尼克只好將球丟到樹叢裡,而凱文跟安迪假裝找球。這時老奶奶拖著緩慢的腳步走過二壘、三壘,然後走向本壘。凱文於是把球撿起來丟向外野的看台。格爾森奶奶越過本壘板,振臂歡呼勝利,大家都為她鼓掌喝采。

格爾森奶奶說:「謝謝你們」。然後她就往自己家的方向走,半途又停下來回過頭說:「你們這些小鬼最好快回去打球,你們要多多練習啊!」

Lesson 8　地球季節的循環　P. 33

地球的運轉導致季節的變化。一年中有春、夏、秋、冬四季,因為地球的自轉與公轉,在同一個時間不同的地方有不同的季節。

四季如何產生

地球自轉一圈是一天,但是地球的軸心並沒有垂直,而是略微傾斜的,所以地球本身也有些傾斜。

地球繞著太陽運轉一圈是一年,稱作公轉。
由於地球是傾斜的,所以太陽的光線會直射到不同的地方,而陽光直射的地方取決於地球的自轉與公轉。地球的自轉與公轉造成當地球上有些地方是白天時,有些地方則是夜晚。

Lesson 9　消防員　P. 37

消防員很忙碌,不論日夜,他們都有可能會被召喚至火場救火,他們必須隨時為緊急情況做好準備。有些消防員有時會住在消防局的宿舍裡,裡頭有床、浴室、廚房,甚至還有休閒娛樂廳。如果晚上沒有火災發生,他們就能休息就寢。消防員在消防局執勤時要檢查救火裝備與消防車,他們會檢查消防水帶上的瞄子,確定運作正常;也會檢查消防車的引擎,確定水箱是否有水、油箱是否有油、輪胎是否有氣。

消防員除了救火之外,還必須處理各種緊急狀況。有時消防員要幫忙需要緊急就醫的民眾;有時要解救受困或有危險的人;有時得清理火場或其他災難現場;有時要在地震後、可怕的暴風雨後或車禍發生後協助民眾。消防員也要花數小時進行火災的防災講習。

即使沒有火災發生,消防員也總是忙個不停。他們要到學校教導學童用火的安全；進修念書保持工作專業度；練習滅火，在火災發生時，才能隨時上場救火。此外，消防員也要到當地公司行號進行消防安檢，確保企業員工和顧客的安全。

消防員回到消防局後，要輪流煮飯和做雜事。有時他們也會為來賓導覽解說消防局裡的設施，展示消防車上的配備，甚至還會開啟消防車的警笛聲呢！

Lesson 10 簡單的預算 P. 40

讓我們來看看這筆簡單的收支預算。Sam 每個星期可以領到 5 美元的零用錢。她每星期幫鄰居劉太太打理花園，可以賺到 15.50 美元。這兩筆錢就是她的收入。而 Sam 的花費包括了每星期看電影的 9.50 美元，還有每星期外食的 5 美元。一個星期過後，Sam 還剩下 6 美元，這些全都會存到她的戶頭裡。那麼你該怎麼編列你的預算呢？

第一步和 Sam 做的事情一樣——記錄你的收入與支出。你要在筆記本上記下你的所得與開銷，並持續記錄幾個星期。這麼做能讓你了解你每星期的金錢流動。

接下來你要未雨綢繆。想想你存錢的目的是什麼。知道自己存錢的目的後，你就能提早幾個星期做規劃。在「收入」欄列出你可以賺多少錢，包括你的零用錢或是額外為家裡做家事所賺的錢。然後在「支出」欄列出你可能會花的錢，包括買東西吃的錢、看電影跟買 CD 的錢，看你做那些消費。

在列這份預算清單時，之前在筆記本上記的資料能幫你很大的忙。現在，把收入欄所有的收入加起來，這就是你的總收入；把支出欄的費用加起來，這就是你的總支出。然後將總收入減去總支出，你就會知道每個星期結束後，你還剩下多少錢，而這些錢就可以存進你的戶頭裡。

Lesson 11 物質的狀態 P. 44

物質有三態：固態、液態、氣態。所有的物質都是以其中的任何一態或是三態的形式存在。

固態

水呈現固態時，可以在上面溜冰，也可以把它放進飲料裡用來冷卻飲料，我們稱為「冰塊」。

液態

水呈現液態時，可以在裡面游泳、可以拿來飲用、洗澡，或是澆花，還能裝滿魚缸。

氣態

水呈現氣態時，叫做「蒸汽」或「水蒸汽」，也就是雲的狀態。水蒸氣決不會留在你家狗狗的碗裡。水壺或熱咖啡上方冉冉升起的熱氣就是水蒸汽。

物質能在不同的溫度下，會從某種狀態改變成另一種狀態。舉例來說，物質可能會溶化或蒸發。不過，即使物質狀態改變了，其分子結構仍維持不變，不會隨著狀態改變而變化。也就是說，無論冰塊、水或蒸汽，它們的水分子結構都是一樣的。

Lesson 12 Tia 與霸凌者 P. 48

Tia 十一歲了，但以她這年紀來說，她的身形算是相當嬌小，而且她家每個人都很高大，所以 Tia 希望不久後她也會長高。

Tia 學校裡有個女生很喜歡欺負她。她會拿走 Tia 午餐裡的食物，然後一口吃掉；她會折斷 Tia 的鉛筆、把她的功課撕掉；她也會找其他的小孩一塊嘲笑 Tia。但是 Tia 卻從來沒跟老師或父母說過她被霸凌的事，因為她覺得很羞愧。

那年夏天，Tia 不斷地長高。到了新學期，她變成班上最高的小孩，甚至比欺負她的女孩還要高。她現在能拿走那個女孩的午餐，然後一口吃掉；也能折斷那個女孩的鉛筆、把她的功課撕掉。但是 Tia 沒有這麼做。她的朋友問她為什麼，她回答：「因為就算我現在比她高，我也從來沒想要去欺負人。」

過了一段時間，霸凌 Tia 的那個女孩對自己過去做的事感到內疚，並請 Tia 原諒她，之後兩人便成了好朋友。

有一天，班上來了個新同學。這個新同學不喜歡 Tia 的新朋友，不久就開始欺負她。新同學欺負她的方式，就跟她當初欺負 Tia 的做法如出一轍。

Tia 可以讓新同學霸凌她的朋友，她可以告訴自己：「也要讓她知道被人家欺負是什麼樣的感覺，就像當初她欺負我一樣」。不過 Tia 不但沒這麼做，她還告訴新同學不要再找她朋友的麻煩。新來的女生很怕 Tia，所以她就不再欺負她的朋友。

Tia 的朋友知道 Tia 為她做了什麼事後，她很高興有 Tia 這樣的朋友，而 Tia 也很高興她能當別人的朋友，而不是霸凌者。

Lesson 13　過去與現在的家庭　P. 53

很久以前，人們都是在城市或鄉鎮裡居住與工作。小孩平常要讀書、做家事，有得玩的時候就玩。全家人一塊吃飯、一起上教堂，互相照拂。

過去的家庭與現在的家庭，並沒有太大的差別。最重要的地方還是一樣，像是家人會彼此相互照顧、關愛。不過有些地方卻有些不同。

很久以前，大人整天都忙著工作。許多男人是農夫，他們要照料穀物與牲畜、負責修繕，並且提供食物給家人。女人則處理家務、照顧小孩、料理三餐、打掃家裡、縫補衣物，還要紡紗。

現今社會的大人也很努力工作。但是他們通常不會工作這麼長的時間，有更多的時間放假、休息。商店與新發明也讓我們的生活更加便利，舉例來說，大部分的人都是在商店採買食物、衣服。有些人會離鄉工作，與自己組成的家庭共度餘生。有些人則選擇在家工作，同時照顧家人。

Lesson 14　沙漠　P. 57

什麼是沙漠？

沙漠就是雨量稀少，白天絕大多數時間都是高溫的陸地區域。

沙漠每年的降雨量不到 10 英吋（25.4 公分），地面通常乾燥。有的時候沙漠下起雨來，陽光的熱度又會將大部分的水曬乾，這就叫做「蒸發」。

造成蒸發的另一個原因是日夜溫差大。沙漠的夜晚非常寒冷，這是因為地表上的沙子在晚上散熱，沙子散熱快，所以沙漠裡的溫度會驟降。白天，沙子會吸收陽光的熱氣，因此沙漠日間的溫度會高達華氏 130 度（攝氏 54 度）。這有多熱

呢？一般人的舒適溫度大約是華氏 70 度（攝氏 21 度），而沙漠的溫度幾乎是這個的兩倍！

沙漠如何形成？

許多沙漠的形成是因為高山阻隔了濕氣的流動。雨、雪都會降落在山上，等大氣流動到沙漠時，早已變得乾燥，無水可降。

有些沙漠形成的原因是離水體太遙遠。大氣從湖泊與海洋吸收水氣，但是早在抵達沙漠前，大氣中的雨就已經陸續降完了，水氣沒有辦法帶到那麼遠。

Lesson 15　女太空人莎莉 · 萊德　P. 61

只有特別的人才能當太空人。要當太空人必須身強體壯，學習力強，擅長數學、科學，還要懂得如何解決問題。這些人還要有成功的欲望，並且與他人合作達成目標。在這些特別的人當中，有個人叫做莎莉 · 萊德（Sally Ride）。

莎莉 · 萊德於 1951 年 5 月 26 日在加州洛杉磯出生。她從小就做過各式各樣的事，她跟男生一起踢足球、打棒球，而男生通常也只會讓她這個女生加入。莎莉的媽媽要她打網球，她就努力把網球打到一流。讀高中的時候，她碰到了一個老師鼓勵她當科學家。

上大學後，莎莉最喜歡做的兩件事就是打網球跟研究科學。她原本有機會成為專業的網球選手，可是她選擇走上科學的路。之後莎莉到史丹佛大學深造，她在那裡看到美國國家航空暨太空總署（NASA）的廣告，NASA 正在招募年輕的科學家當太空人。

這個廣告是莎莉人生中的轉捩點。那年有 8,000 多人向美國航太總署提出申請，只有 35 人脫穎而出，莎莉就是其中之一。在莎莉辛勤工作、努力讀書的同時，她也接受太空人的訓練。美國航太總署的人都很看重她。而她的付出在 1982 年終於有所回報，她獲選為第七次太空梭任務的太空人。莎莉 · 萊德是第一個飛到外太空的美籍女性。

在挑戰者號上，她負責操作類似機器人手臂的器械。這個機器手臂能協助太空人在衛星上工作。她證明了不論性別，她都是最適合做這項工作的人。莎莉也曾出過 1984 年挑戰者號的太空任務。

然而 1986 年卻發生了悲劇，這是挑戰者號第十次執行太空任務，太空梭卻在起飛後隨即爆炸，機上七位太空人全都不幸罹難，而莎莉是事故調查小組的一員。不久後，她離開太空計畫，到史丹佛大學工作。

莎莉‧萊德立志要盡力做到最好，成為一流的人才。她是全世界年輕人的模範，因為她努力追尋、達成自己的夢想。莎莉‧萊德為自己在太空探索的歷史中，贏得一席之地。

Lesson 16　非洲藝術 P.64

非洲藝術有著悠遠流長的歷史，最古老的藝術品可追溯至西元前 6,000 年。這些藝術品包括繪畫與雕飾，展現出非洲民族文化的多樣性，他們有許多不同型態的傳統藝術，包括紡織品與首飾。

非洲織品藝術

非洲人喜歡鮮豔的色彩、圖案與質地，這些在他們的生活中隨處可見。在雨林地帶，樹幹從樹上砍下來後，會經過浸泡與槌擊，然後做成布料，之後再用布料製作衣物。姆布蒂（Mbuti）部落的女人從植物提煉出染料，並用染料在布上作畫。其他的部落，則是將植物纖維剝下來染，然後再織成布。古埃及人使用亞麻植物上的纖維，織成質地細緻的白布，稱為「麻布」。

「肯特」（Kente）是迦納（Ghana）部落所織造的華麗織品。他們以拉菲草（乾草）的纖維混合成絲後，織成布料，先在在織布機上將布織成長條狀，然後再將這些長條狀的布拼織成品。織品的花樣繁複，每種圖案都有名稱，有其象徵意義。

非洲首飾

首飾在非洲扮演了很重要的角色。不論女人、男人或小孩，他們的身上都會配帶飾品。首飾有許多種設計，可以戴在身上各個地方。每個部落的首飾都有其特殊的意涵，有些首飾只能在像婚禮這樣的特殊場合配戴；有些首飾則用來餽贈，像是友誼手環。每一件首飾都是配戴者財富與地位的展現。

許多傳統素材都能拿來製成首飾，包括動物的皮毛、貝殼、象牙、玻璃等。金屬也可用來製成首飾，可利用的金屬有金、錫、銅、銀等。

你也許還有興趣認識非洲其他類型的藝術品，例如雕刻、傢俱與陶器。

Lesson 17　捍衛改革 P.69

1920 年，女人取得壓倒性的勝利。這一年，女人贏得了投票權之戰 —— 女人總算可以投票了。當時有位女性打破所有的規則，以總統夫人之名，為眾人平等而戰。她的名字就叫做愛莉諾‧羅斯福（Eleanor Roosevelt）。

愛莉諾‧羅斯福

在 1930 年代，許多非裔美國人並未受到公平地對待。愛莉諾看到那些非裔美國人無法與白人上同樣的學校，不能一塊吃飯，有些鄉鎮甚至禁止他們投票。

身為第一夫人，愛莉諾知道她必須做些甚麼，因此她要求從政者制定公民權，希望所有人都擁有相同的權利，而她從未放棄過努力。

幫助瑪莉安‧安德生

瑪莉安‧安德生（Marian Anderson）在 1930 年代是相當知名的女歌手。她的歌喉美妙動聽，歌唱事業也相當成功。安德生本來計畫要在華盛頓特區某個熱門地點獻唱，可是她卻被告知她不能在那裡唱歌，因為她是非裔美國人。愛莉諾‧羅斯福對這件事很生氣，所以她為安德生想了個辦法，讓她在華盛頓特區的其他地方唱歌，那個特殊的地點就是林肯紀念堂。安德生在超過 75,000 人的面前獻唱，最後她以一曲＜美國＞結束這場演唱會。那首歌有一句是這麼唱的：「讓自由之聲響徹每座山腰」。對在場的每個人來說，這是特別的一刻。

Lesson 18　第三章：棒球界的偉人 —— 羅伯特‧克萊門提 P.73

羅伯特‧克萊門提（Robert Clemente）熱愛打棒球。他在波多黎各的卡羅萊納長大，從小他就抓緊每個可以打棒球的機會。他會一邊聽收音機，手裡一邊捏著球來強化投球手臂的肌力。他還會對著牆壁丟皮球來訓練接球。他跟朋友買不起真正的棒球，就自己動手做。他們拿舊的高爾夫球、繩子跟膠帶來做專屬棒球。

隨著羅伯特的年齡漸長，他更是勤加練習，也因此成了比別人更強的棒球運動員。那時布魯克林道奇隊希望羅伯特加入他們的球隊，但是羅伯特的爸爸說他得先完成學業。畢業後，羅伯特到加拿大的蒙特婁，在小聯盟打球。有些職業球隊會去看他打球，不久匹茲堡海盜隊就要他擔任球隊的右外野手，而羅伯特也接受了。

在羅伯特為海盜隊效力期間，該隊贏得了兩次世界大賽的冠軍，而他是 1971 年世界大賽最有價值的球員。在他的棒球生涯中，他擊出 3,000 多支安打。身為冠軍，羅伯特卻從來沒忘記他的球迷。賽後，他沒有與隊員一起去狂歡，而是留下來感謝球迷對他的支持。羅伯特捐錢給有需要的人，花時間探訪生病的孩童。當尼加拉瓜遭地震侵襲，他花了整個聖誕節假期為受災者募資。1972 年 12 月 31 日，他準備從波多黎各搭飛機前往尼加拉瓜遞送物資。然而飛機起飛不久後就發生空難了，羅伯特與機上乘客全數罹難。

許多人都非常感懷羅伯特。他去世三個月後，就獲選進入美國棒球名人堂。羅伯特的父親希望他能當個堂堂正正的好人，而羅伯特的所作所為也證明了他是位偉人。

Lesson 19 蓋鳥舍 P. 76

確定你的鳥舍組件裡有這些零件：

2 片屋頂板
1 片前板，板上有兩個洞跟尖尖的上端
1 片後板，板子上端要尖尖的
1 根圓形木桿
2 片側板
1 片底板
1 條金屬鏈
兩個螺絲釘
1 條木膠

步驟說明：

1. 將底板平放。把兩片側板以 90 度直角黏在底板的兩邊。
2. 將前、後板與這三塊木板黏在一起。
3. 在適當的位置黏上兩片屋頂板。之後將黏好的鳥舍閒置一晚，直到木膠變乾。
4. 將圓桿推進鳥舍前板的小圓洞裡。
5. 將螺絲釘鎖進兩個事先鑽好的洞裡，並用金屬鏈綁住屋頂。
6. 在樹下或是你家的屋簷下找個隱蔽的地點，把

鳥舍掛上去。不久後，你就會有一窩快樂的鳥兒在那裡築巢。

7. 之後就能用望遠鏡觀望快樂的鳥兒一家。

Lesson 20 楓糖樹 P. 81

楓糖樹是一種很棒的樹。楓糖漿和楓糖都是從楓糖樹的樹液提煉而成，其樹幹能用來製作漂亮的傢俱和櫃子，此外楓糖樹也能提供不錯的樹蔭遮陽。人們會在房子的周圍種植楓糖樹，也會把樹種在街道的兩旁。

秋天時，楓糖樹的葉子會轉為鮮豔的黃色、橘色或是深紅色，彷彿有人拿把大刷子粉刷過那些葉子般。冬天時，樹葉紛紛掉落，成了光禿禿的樹。

楓糖樹的樹皮呈灰色，而且很容易剝落。它的籽常是鳥兒、松鼠等小動物的食物。

楓糖樹可長到 75 到 100 英呎高（22.9 到 30.4 公尺）。楓樹有 60 多種不同的品種，黑楓、紅楓跟銀楓只不過是其中的幾種。但是如果你想要在院子裡種一棵楓樹，那麼就種楓糖樹吧！

Lesson 21 螞蟻與蛹 P. 85

有一隻螞蟻在陽光下跑來跑去尋找食物，這時牠發現一個即將羽化成蝶的蛹。蛹動了動尾部，這立刻吸引了螞蟻的注意，螞蟻還是第一次看到活著的蛹。螞蟻說：「可憐的東西！你的命運真悲慘！我可以隨心所欲地跑來跑去。如果我想的話，我還可以爬上那最高的樹。而你卻被困在自己的殼裡，頂多只能動動你的關節，或是你那滿是鱗片的狹翅鬚。」蛹聽到了螞蟻說的話，可是牠卻無意回應。

幾天後，螞蟻又經過那裡。但是這次，那裡只剩下一個空殼。螞蟻納悶地想著蛹裡頭的東西去哪兒時，突然間牠感覺到上方有隻美麗的蝴蝶遮住了灑在自己身上的陽光，牠振翅而扇動的風吹到了自己的身上。

「看看我，你這個更可憐的傢伙」帝王蝶說，「盡管吹噓你那能跑又能爬的本事吧！但我一點也不想聽。」說完，蝴蝶就升空飛去。牠很快地就永遠從螞蟻的視線中失去蹤影。

這個寓言故事告訴我們：不可以只看表象。

Lesson 22　神奇的夜晚　P. 88

　　四年級所有班級的孩子邀請您，

茲臨觀賞本學年度的第一場戲劇表演。

　　孩子們想出了獨一無二的好點子。

那就是以音樂劇演出古典名著《愛麗絲夢遊仙境》。

　　本書乃路易士・卡洛於 1865 年首度創作。

本劇將於本週六晚間七點在兒童劇場為您隆重呈現。

這齣音樂劇的主角不是愛麗絲，而是艾莉西亞。在我們的版本中，她夢到她尾隨她的貓咪跑進了臥室的衣櫥裡。可是她一進到衣櫥裡，卻驚訝得不敢相信眼前所見的一切。貓咪帶領她走進幻想與冒險的世界。在這個充滿神奇的地方，她看到的動物跟樹都會說話。她發現了一條秘密通道，而且最棒的是，她見到了所有的好朋友，只不過她的好朋友們也全都是動物！有趣的故事就此展開！

四年級每班同學都參與了歌曲創作（老師們也幫了一些忙），戲服也都是學生們自己做的，所以您千萬不可錯過！本劇是由四年級的老師特倫斯・伯德老師指導。他曾在 Rossmoor 市民輕歌劇裡演出，這是他第十次指導戲劇表演。

Lesson 23　為什麼會肚子餓　P. 93

你曾經想過你為什麼會肚子餓嗎？這是因為你的胃告訴你該吃些東西了。胃裡面沒有食物時，胃就會收縮，收縮的意思就是擠在一起。空腹時，胃每分鐘大約會收縮三次。如果你還是沒進食，收縮的頻率就會開始增加。這時你的胃會傳送訊息到你的大腦，告訴大腦說：「喂！我這裡需要食物。快點送過來！」

大腦裡會讓你感覺飢餓的部分叫做「食慾調節中樞」。這個部分也會在你吃飽時，告訴你停下來，別再吃了。無人確切知道食慾調節中樞到底是怎麼運作，有些人認為它跟家裡的恆溫器作用相同。當你血液裡的葡萄糖降低時，你的胃就會大叫：「該吃東西了！」當你血液裡的葡萄糖升高時，你的胃就會說：「別再吃了，你已經吃飽了。」

你知道進食的心情會影響到胃裡的食物嗎？如果用餐時心情愉快，食物很快就會被消化，這表示食物會轉換成能量。可是如果用餐時生氣或難過，食物就會待在胃裡不動，那麼你就會覺得胃不舒服。這給我們什麼樣的啟示呢？最好是快樂地進食，不要在生氣或難過時吃東西！

Lesson 24　為公民權而抗爭　P. 97

在 1955 年之前，只有律師會出面反對種族隔離政策。想要從根本上改變，就必須在法庭外發生某件大事。那年的 12 月 1 日，阿拉巴馬州的蒙哥馬利就發生了一件大事。

那天，有輛公車上擠滿了乘客。當時的人認為非裔美國人應該要讓位給白人坐。羅莎・帕克斯（Rosa Parks）是位非裔美國人，可是這天她卻沒有讓位給白人坐，也因此遭警察逮捕、囚禁。

但是他們不知道帕克斯在當地的全國有色人種協會（NAACP）工作。當地的民權領袖喬安・羅賓遜（Jo Ann Robinson）想出了一個計劃：她將傳單分發給住在該市所有的非裔美國人，傳單上寫著「拒搭公車」。羅賓遜原以為這項抗爭一天就會結束了，沒想到卻持續了一年的時間。

這是個和平的抗議行動，而且前所未見。這是第一次不是由律師出面為非裔美國人的權利據以力爭，而是所有市民的自發之舉。非裔美國人此時明白，想要改變法律就必須團結一致。

Lesson 25　契沙比克灣　P. 100

位於美國東部海陸交會之處的契沙比克灣是個風景秀麗的地方。這個大海灣的四面環繞著馬里蘭州、維吉尼亞州與大西洋。四方的旅客前來此地揚帆、垂釣和觀光。

這座海灣不僅是絕佳的觀光度假勝地，還是世界最負盛名的濱海溼地之一。契沙比克灣的海岸線長而崎嶇，極易形成溼地。河流的支流在內陸延伸，這些支流不斷地灌溉溼地、餵養在那裡生活的動植物。

契沙比克灣是許多動植物的棲息地，其中腹地最廣的就是溼地。在溼地，不論水面上或水面下都可找到動植物的蹤跡。溼地也分不同的類型，有些溼地大多數是樹木，只有少數是灌木叢；有些溼地則大多是草地與灌木叢，只有少量的樹木，而契沙比克灣的溼地則兩者皆具。

什麼樣的條件才能讓一塊地變成溼地呢？溼地有一些關鍵特色。當然，第一個特色是水。溼地上有淺水，而契沙比克灣的淡水溼地只有幾英呎深。潮間溼地有淺有深，取決於潮汐的大小。

溼地是一些植物的大本營，這類植物終年生長在水中或潮溼的土壤裡。一旦植物或樹木凋謝枯死便掉到水中，開始腐化。濕地的動物、昆蟲、細菌便以這些腐爛的物質為食物。

溼地上的動物也能夠在這樣的環境條件下生存，牠們的身體構造有助於其在水裡活動與生活。

Lesson 26 埃及的女法老 —— 哈姬蘇女王 P. 105

許多人認為哈姬蘇（Hatshepsut）是埃及歷史上最偉大的女性。她所處的時代稱為「新王國」。在她之前，從未有女性統治過埃及。

大約在西元前 1518 年，圖特摩斯一世繼位為王。國王與王后育有二子、二女，但是只有一個孩子活到成年，那個孩子就是哈姬蘇。在哈姬蘇十幾歲的時候，她父親便過世了。

哈姬蘇是個領導慾強烈的年輕女子。她能讀能寫，也喜歡學習新知。她看著父親怎麼當法老王治理埃及，而她對如何讓埃及繁榮興盛也有自己的一套看法。

圖特摩斯一世和王妃育有一子，圖特摩斯二世即繼位新法老王。新任法老王年僅八歲，因此哈姬蘇擔任攝政王長達十年之久。攝政王是在法老王過於年幼或纏綿病榻時，代為處理政務的人。哈姬蘇意志堅定而聰慧，國家大事由她來決策，而祭司與其他首長則負責執行。

圖特摩斯二世年紀輕輕就死了。西元前 1504 年左右，圖特摩斯三世成為法老王，不過他那時還只是個小嬰兒。所以哈姬蘇又再度當上了攝政王。大約七年後，哈姬蘇便自行稱王，統治埃及長達 22 年之久。她興建的紀念碑與藝術作品比任何一位埃及女王都還要多。而且，在她統治之下，當代的埃及文明無比興盛強大。

Lesson 27 蒐集資料 P. 109

計算人口數

政府會蒐集住在該國人民的資料，這就是所謂的戶口普查，大約每十年會進行一次。

人口普查蒐集來的資料很重要，這些資料能讓政府了解城市與鄉鎮的人口數，有助於政府進行學校的規劃或是道路的興建，也能讓政府決定是否需要增建地鐵或加派公車。

蒐集人口普查資料

現在大多數的人都是透過電子郵件收到人口普查的問卷調查表，不過有些人收到後沒有回信。如果人口普查的問卷調查表沒有被寄回，負責的工作人員為了取得所需的資料，就會以電話或到府訪查的方式進行人口普查。

一份資料，多種用途

許多報告都需要用到人口普查的資料，如人口及居住調查報告，有時候「多少學生到學校註冊」的報告也需要用到人口普查的資料。

規劃學校的人使用人口普查的資料，來了解社區與城鎮。他們可以藉此預測有多少學生即將入學，這份資料也告訴他們什麼時候需要興建新的學校。

就連救難人員也會用到人口普查的資料。他們可以從資料中得知，若發生緊急意外事故時，有多少人需要救援。

Lesson 28 全年制學校教育 P. 113

學校放的暑假實在太長了。等學生放完暑假，回到學校上課後，他們不但必須複習所有學過的知識，還得重新適應學校上下課的時間表。

在傳統的學年制訂定之初，大多數人都是住在鄉間農莊裡。學生放暑假是因為他們必須幫忙家裡收割農作物。如今，大多數人都不住在農場，所以學生不需要整個夏天都放假。

我建議應該要有更多的學校實施全年制教育。全年制教育的假期分散在整個學年度，學生在校上課的天數仍然是相同的，只不過放假的時間分散些罷了，原本在夏天的時候有兩個月的假期，可能改成只有一個月，所以學生還是可以參加夏令營，放他們的暑假。如此一來，學生跟老師在學年期間也比較不會精疲力竭，因為在學年期間有假可以放。

關於實施全年制學校教育是否能增進學生的學業成就，此項研究的結果是毀譽參半。有些研究顯示是肯定的，然而有些研究卻持相反的意見。儘管如此，我仍然認為全年制學校教育是較佳的制度，我覺得這個制度能解決暑假過長的問題。

Lesson 29 芭蕾舞 P. 117

很久很久以前，第一場正統的芭蕾舞在法國上演。芭蕾舞是一種展現特殊肢體動作的舞蹈，而且通常具有故事性。芭蕾舞源自於義大利，可是第一間芭蕾舞舞蹈學校卻是在法國成立的，而且芭蕾舞的用語也全是法文。法國人將芭蕾舞變成我們現在所知道的美麗表演藝術。

跳芭蕾舞的女舞者叫做 ballerinas，男芭蕾舞者則叫做 danseurs。他們都是身輕體健的舞者，從四、五歲起就要開始接受芭蕾舞的訓練課程，包含音樂和芭蕾的基本舞姿等。到了十一、二歲時，這些芭蕾舞者每天都要上課，而且必須非常努力學習。有些舞者有野心、有天賦，可是也要有極佳的運氣才有機會進入職業芭蕾舞團。此時舞者年約十七、八歲，有的年紀甚至更大。

芭蕾舞者即使是在閒暇時，也念念不忘芭蕾舞。他們想盡辦法維持身材健美，真的是非常有運動家的風範。他們喜歡芭蕾舞那種能控制自己身體的感覺，這讓他們得以做出非常困難的動作或姿勢，跳出若非芭蕾舞者絕對做不到的曼妙舞姿。

Lesson 30 啄木鳥與獅子 P. 121

源自《More Jataka Tales》一書
由 Ellen C. Babbitt 重述

有一天，獅子正大快朵頤地吃著晚餐時，一根骨頭卡到喉嚨。獅子痛得不得了，讓牠沒辦法繼續把晚餐吃完。牠走來走去，走來走去，還一邊痛苦地咆哮著。

有一隻啄木鳥站在附近的樹枝上，聽到獅子的怒吼聲，她說：「獅子大哥，什麼事讓你這麼煩惱呢？」獅子告訴啄木鳥牠哪裡不舒服，然後啄木鳥回答說：「獅子大哥，我可以幫你把喉嚨裡的骨頭拿出來，可是我不敢把我的頭放進你的嘴裡，因為我怕你會吃了我，我就再也出不來了。」

「哦，啄木鳥，別怕，」獅子說，「我不會吃了妳。如果可以的話，請救我一命吧！」

「我看看我要怎麼幫你的忙，」啄木鳥命令說，「張大嘴。」獅子欣然從命。但是啄木鳥自言自語地說：「誰知道這隻獅子會做出什麼事出來？我想我還是小心為上。」

所以啄木鳥把一根樹枝架在獅子的上下顎之間，這樣獅子的嘴巴就閉不起來了。啄木鳥這才跳進獅子的嘴裡，用牠的鳥喙啄骨頭的一端。就在牠第二次嘗試啄那根骨頭時，骨頭就掉出來了。啄木鳥接著跳出獅子的嘴，並把卡在獅子兩顎間的樹枝啄倒，獅子也能把嘴巴閉上了。牠馬上就覺得舒服多了，可是牠卻連一句感謝的話都沒有對啄木鳥說。

之後的某個夏天，啄木鳥對獅子說：「我要你幫我做某件事。」

「幫妳做件事？」獅子冷語道，「妳的意思是要我幫妳做更多的事嗎？我已經幫了妳一個大忙！別忘了，妳曾經在我的嘴巴裡，是我讓妳活著走出我的嘴巴，別再妄想要我幫妳任何事情。」

啄木鳥不發一語，但從這天起她就離獅子遠遠地。

第三章 海底火山 P.124

地球上有幾座最大的火山群是我們人類從未見過的。因為這些火山隱藏在深海之中，我們必須潛入海中 1.5 英里才能看到這些火山。我們稱這一連串的海底火山為「中洋脊」。

「中洋脊」是地球上最大的山脈，長逾 30,000 英里，寬幾乎達 500 英里。中洋脊中有許多座山巒與火山群，曲折蜿蜒於五大洲之間的深海中，就像棒球上面的接縫線般，彎彎曲曲地繞著地球。這表示世界到處都有海底山脈與火山群。每天幾乎至少會有一座海底火山爆發。超級炙熱的熔岩漿從火山口噴發而出，沿著火山滾滾向下流到海底。

海底的地形一直在變化。超級炙熱的熔岩漿從地球內部噴出，經過冷卻形成了岩石，這些熔岩岩石便一層層地堆積起來。經過數百萬年後，這些熔岩使海底擴張。當海底擴張時，熔岩就會擠壓周圍的陸地。一百萬年前的地球與今日的地球看起來大不相同。從現在開始的一百萬年後，地球的變化將會更加巨大。

肅清每個社區 P.126

新上任的總統應該要開始處理汙染的問題，以及汙染如何毒害環境的議題。在收入較低的地區，時常可見那些會造成危害的化工廠與垃圾場，因為當地的居民並未參與決策。

空氣汙染，或者說煙霧汙染，是汽車和卡車所造成的。降下的酸雨流入魚兒生存的湖泊裡，落入植物林立的森林中。許多河流和湖泊受到化學製品的汙染。汽車車流與飛機的聲音導致了噪音汙染。

我們的新總統應該要先處理這類的汙染問題，因為這些汙染影響了許多小孩的生活，引發氣喘、癌症，以及其他的疾病。

Jullisa T.，四年級

解決遊民的問題 P.126

有太多人到處流浪，他們沒有食物，而且大多數都是小孩子。許多遊民都是來自貧窮的工人階級。這表示他們有工作，卻無法養家，付不出房租。還有另一件事情令我感到震驚，我發現有超過三百萬人居無定所，一年之中至少有一晚是沒地方可去。

政府應該教育人民了解這些遊民。這麼做應該可以減少大家對遊民的歧視。我們需要美國的總統提供就業方案，讓他們做薪水高的工作。新上任的總統甚至可以考慮再次提高基本工資。

Lucas V.，五年級

烏鴉與水瓶 P.128

很久以前，有一隻口非常渴的烏鴉，在飛經田園鄉間時，看到房子的附近有一個老舊的水瓶。

牠往下飛，心中想著：「那個瓶子裡也許會有水。」

烏鴉降落在黑金相間的容器旁，然後往水瓶裡一看。水瓶裡有水，只不過是在瓶底。牠將鳥喙探進瓶子裡，可是瓶子太高了，牠喝不到水。此時烈陽當空高掛，烏鴉感到更渴了。

「如果我還喝不到水，我會渴死的！」牠聲音沙啞地說。

牠一定要喝到水，可是牠該怎麼做才能喝到瓶子裡的水呢？如果牠把瓶子弄倒了，水就會流到地上。牠四下環顧，設法找出能從瓶子裡喝到水的方法。這時，牠看到了地上的小石子。

烏鴉突然間想到了一個辦法。牠用鳥喙撿起小石子，然後把小石子丟進水瓶裡。小石子撲通地一聲碰觸到了水面，烏鴉知道這個方法是行得通的。牠趕緊收集更多的小石子，然後一個接一個地丟進水瓶裡，水開始慢慢地上升。等水升到夠高，烏鴉就把鳥喙伸進水瓶，喝著裡頭清涼的水，久久不停。

這個寓言故事告訴我們：需要為發明之母！

颶風之內 P.130

暴風雨的中心稱之為「風眼」。風眼是一片平靜無風的圓狀範圍，快速旋轉的強風圍繞著風眼。最強烈的旋風形成了風眼的內壁，而風眼的周圍則有巨雲盤繞，巨雲引起大雨和閃電。

FUN 學美國英語 閱讀寫作 課本

AMERICAN SCHOOL TEXTBOOK

GRADE **1**
MP3 ◀))

Reading & Writing

作者 Christine Dugan / Leslie Huber / Margot Kinberg, 等　譯者 黃詩韻

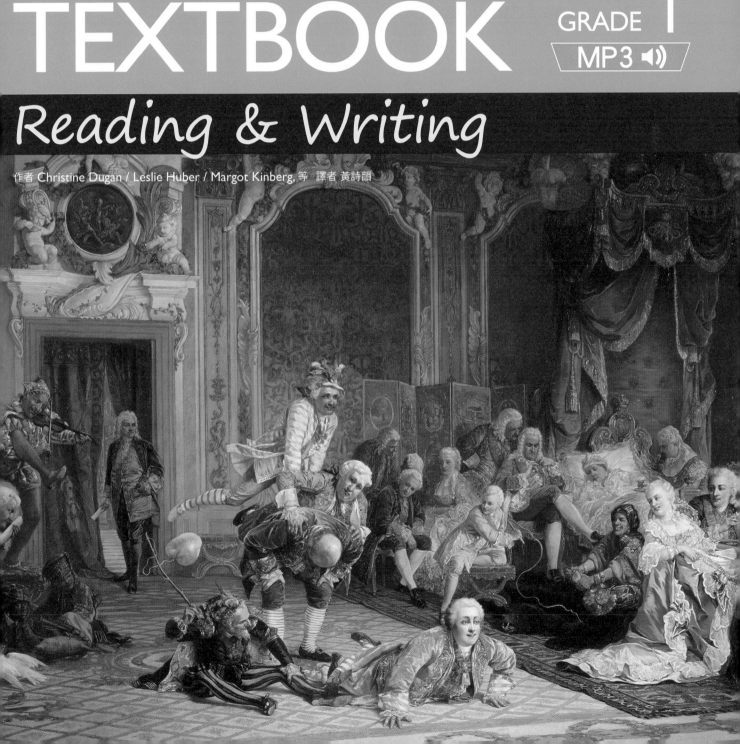

FUN 學美國英語 閱讀寫作 課本 1
American School Textbook: Reading & Writing

作　　者	Christine Dugan / Leslie Huber / Margot Kinberg / Miriam Meyers / Inga Townsend
審　　定	Judy Majewski
譯　　者	黃詩韻
編　　輯	呂紹柔

封面設計	王怡真／李燕青
內文排版	田慧盈／李燕青
製程管理	洪巧玲
出 版 者	寂天文化事業股份有限公司
電　　話	+886-(0)2-2365-9739
傳　　真	+886-(0)2-2365-9835
網　　址	www.icosmos.com.tw
讀者服務	onlineservice@icosmos.com.tw
出版日期	2019 年 9 月 初版再刷　(080103)

郵撥帳號　1998620-0　　寂天文化事業股份有限公司

・劃撥金額 600（含）元以上者，郵資免費。

・訂購金額 600 元以下者，加收 65 元運費。

【若有破損，請寄回更換，謝謝。】

HOW TO USE THIS BOOK

The **Lesson Number** and **Reading Skill** are clearly identified.

The **Reading Tip** provides guidance for reading each lesson.

The **Skill Overview** provides background information about the skill focus for the lesson.

Reading Passage

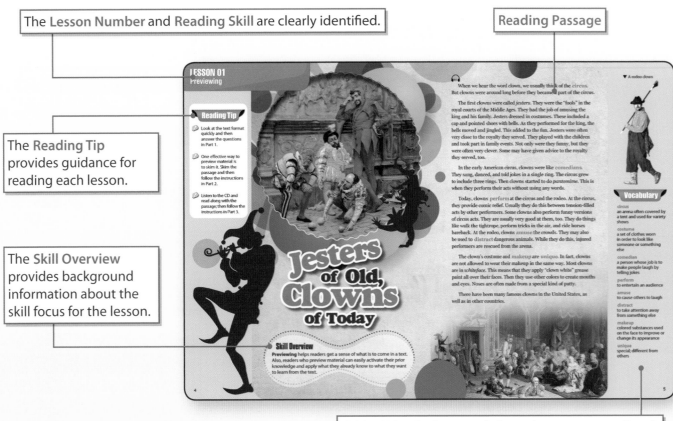

Critical Vocabulary words from the passage are listed.

Power Up summarizes the key terminology and ideas for each lesson.

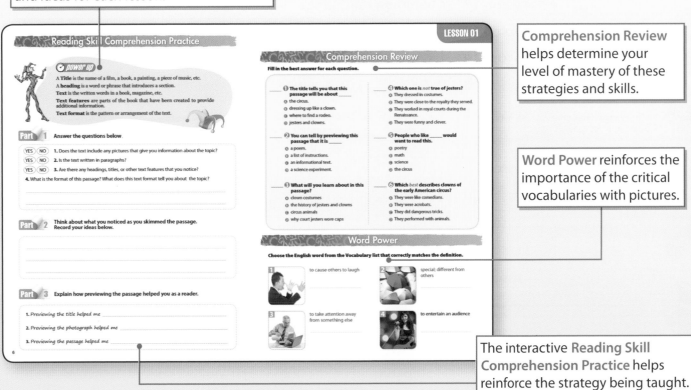

Comprehension Review helps determine your level of mastery of these strategies and skills.

Word Power reinforces the importance of the critical vocabularies with pictures.

The interactive **Reading Skill Comprehension Practice** helps reinforce the strategy being taught.

Contents Chart

Reading Skill	Subject
Previewing	Social Studies ★ History and Geography
Cause and Effect—Plot	Language and Literature
Headings to Determine Main Ideas	Social Studies ★ History and Geography
Main Idea	Science
Compare and Contrast	Social Studies ★ History and Geography
Topic to Predict	Social Studies ★ History and Geography
Character	Language and Literature
Topic Sentences to Determine Main Ideas	Science
Prior Knowledge	Social Studies ★ History and Geography
Sequential Order	Mathematics
Meaning Clues to Predict	Science
Problem and Solution—Plot	Language and Literature
Captions to Determine Main Ideas	Social Studies ★ History and Geography
Graphic Features	Science
Chronological Order	Social Studies ★ History and Geography
Structure to Predict	Visual Arts
Author's Purpose	Social Studies ★ History and Geography
Chapter Titles to Determine Main Ideas	Social Studies ★ History and Geography
Logical Order	Social Studies ★ History and Geography
Fact and Opinion	Science
Monitoring Reading Strategies	Language and Literature
Purpose for Reading	Music
Cause and Effect	Science
Summary Sentences	Social Studies ★ History and Geography
Retelling	Social Studies ★ History and Geography
Selecting Reading Material	Social Studies ★ History and Geography
Typeface	Social Studies ★ History and Geography
Proposition and Support	Social Studies ★ History and Geography
Summarizing	Visual Arts
Questioning	Language and Literature

Reading Tip

- Look at the text format quickly and then answer the questions in Part 1.

- One effective way to preview material is to skim it. Skim the passage and then follow the instructions in Part 2.

- Listen to the CD and read along with the passage; then follow the instructions in Part 3.

Jesters of Old, Clowns of Today

Skill Overview

Previewing helps readers get a sense of what is to come in a text. Also, readers who preview material can easily activate their prior knowledge and apply what they already know to what they want to learn from the text.

When we hear the word clown, we usually think of the **circus**. But clowns were around long before they became a part of the circus.

The first clowns were called *jesters*. They were the "fools" in the royal courts of the Middle Ages. They had the job of amusing the king and his family. Jesters dressed in costumes. These included a cap and pointed shoes with bells. As they performed for the king, the bells moved and jingled. This added to the fun. Jesters were often very close to the royalty they served. They played with the children and took part in family events. Not only were they funny, but they were often very clever. Some may have given advice to the royalty they served, too.

In the early American circus, clowns were like **comedians**. They sang, danced, and told jokes in a single ring. The circus grew to include three rings. Then clowns started to do *pantomime*. This is when they perform their acts without using any words.

Today, clowns **perform** at the circus and the rodeo. At the circus, they provide comic relief. Usually they do this between tension-filled acts by other performers. Some clowns also perform funny versions of circus acts. They are usually very good at them, too. They do things like walk the tightrope, perform tricks in the air, and ride horses bareback. At the rodeo, clowns **amuse** the crowds. They may also be used to **distract** dangerous animals. While they do this, injured performers are rescued from the arena.

The clown's costume and **makeup** are **unique**. In fact, clowns are not allowed to wear their makeup in the same way. Most clowns are in *whiteface*. This means that they apply "clown white" grease paint all over their faces. Then they use other colors to create mouths and eyes. Noses are often made from a special kind of putty.

There have been many famous clowns in the United States, as well as in other countries.

▼ A rodeo clown

Vocabulary

circus
an arena often covered by a tent and used for variety shows

costume
a set of clothes worn in order to look like someone or something else

comedian
a person whose job is to make people laugh by telling jokes

perform
to entertain an audience

amuse
to cause others to laugh

distract
to take attention away from something else

makeup
colored substances used on the face to improve or change its appearance

unique
special; different from others

power up

A **title** is the name of a film, a book, a painting, a piece of music, etc.

A **heading** is a word or phrase that introduces a section.

Text is the written words in a book, magazine, etc.

Text features are parts of the book that have been created to provide additional information.

Text format is the pattern or arrangement of the text.

Part 1 Answer the questions below.

(YES)(NO) **1.** Does the text include any pictures that give you information about the topic?

(YES)(NO) **2.** Is the text written in paragraphs?

(YES)(NO) **3.** Are there any headings, titles, or other text features that you notice?

4. What is the format of this passage? What does this text format tell you about the topic?

_____

_____

Part 2 Think about what you noticed as you skimmed the passage. Record your ideas below.

_____

_____

_____

Part 3 Explain how previewing the passage helped you as a reader.

1. Previewing the title helped me _____

2. Previewing the photograph helped me _____

3. Previewing the passage helped me _____

Comprehension Review

Fill in the best answer for each question.

_____ ❶ **The title tells you that this passage will be about _____**
Ⓐ the circus.
Ⓑ dressing up like a clown.
Ⓒ where to find a rodeo.
Ⓓ jesters and clowns.

_____ ❷ **You can tell by previewing this passage that it is _____**
Ⓐ a poem.
Ⓑ a list of instructions.
Ⓒ an informational text.
Ⓓ a science experiment.

_____ ❸ **What will you learn about in this passage?**
Ⓐ clown costumes
Ⓑ the history of jesters and clowns
Ⓒ circus animals
Ⓓ why court jesters wore caps

_____ ❹ **Which one is _not_ true of jesters?**
Ⓐ They dressed in costumes.
Ⓑ They were close to the royalty they served.
Ⓒ They worked in royal courts during the Renaissance.
Ⓓ They were funny and clever.

_____ ❺ **People who like _____ would want to read this.**
Ⓐ poetry
Ⓑ math
Ⓒ science
Ⓓ the circus

_____ ❻ **Which _best_ describes clowns of the early American circus?**
Ⓐ They were like comedians.
Ⓑ They were acrobats.
Ⓒ They did dangerous tricks.
Ⓓ They performed with animals.

Word Power

Choose the English word from the Vocabulary list that correctly matches the definition.

 1 to cause others to laugh

_____

 2 special; different from others

_____

 3 to take attention away from something else

_____

 4 to entertain an audience

_____

Racing a Tornado

Skill Overview

Cause and effect is a text structure in which the effect happens as a result of the cause. The cause is the event or situation, and the effect is the consequence of the event or situation. Knowing the cause-and-effect pattern in texts can help readers better comprehend what they read.

🎧 02

If we had known what was going to happen, we never would have gotten on our bikes. But it was a perfect day for a long bike ride. Maria and I **set out** at 7 A.M. and didn't stop for lunch until noon. We sat under an oak tree and had a picnic. That's when the day began to change and we started to worry. In the distance, a towering bank of dark clouds **appeared**. We looked at each other. There was no way we could **avoid** that storm.

The weather quickly got worse. The sky was very dark, and the

Vocabulary

- ⭐ **set out**
  to start an activity with a particular aim

- ⭐ **appear**
  to be or come in sight

- **avoid**
  to keep away from

- **colossal**
  very large in size; huge

- **funnel**
  a tubelike form that is wide at the top and narrow at the bottom

- **screech**
  to make a shrill, high-pitched sound

- **bolt**
  to fasten with a bolt

- **roaring**
  a loud noise

trees were bending in the wind. Suddenly, a yellow car pulled up alongside our bikes. The woman at the wheel was Maria's mother. She opened a door and shouted, "Get in!" She looked as frightened as we felt.

We jumped in just as **colossal** chunks of hail began to fall. The car sped away as hailstones bounced off the hood. Maria and I looked back at the dark sky. Maria screamed, "It's a tornado!" The black **funnel** seemed to be getting closer. I was terrified. How could we outrun that monster? Maria's mother turned to us. "Your grandmother's house is not far," she said. "I know she has a storm cellar that we can use for cover." She sped down the road and turned sharply into a narrow driveway. Soon, the car **screeched** to a halt. Maria's mother yelled at us to get inside the storm cellar. We **bolted** through the doors—and not a minute too soon. A **roaring** like a freight train passed over us. Then, suddenly, it was over. We had made it— barely. It was a race we didn't ever want to run again.

A storm cellar

hailstones

A tornado

9

 Cause means **the reason** why something happens.

 Effect means **the result** of a particular influence.

 Plot means **the story** of a book, a film, a play, etc.

 **Part 1** In the first paragraph, the narrator states "But it was a perfect day for a long bike ride." Make a list of at least three effects of this cause.

1. _____

2. _____

3. _____

The plot is also introduced in the first paragraph. The cause and its effects relate to the plot of the passage. Please write a sentence describing the plot.

4. _____

Part 2 In the second paragraph, the narrator says, "The weather quickly got worse." Write two effects of the bad weather.

1. _____

2. _____

Part 3 Finally, the characters see the tornado approaching. In this story, the cause —a tornado coming—is also the problem, or plot. Write three effects of the approaching tornado.

1. _____

2. _____

3. _____

Write a sentence describing the outcome of the story.

4. _____

_____

Comprehension Review

Fill in the best answer for each question.

_____ ❶ **What caused the narrator and Maria to worry?**

Ⓐ a flat bike tire

Ⓑ the changing weather

Ⓒ bees

Ⓓ being lost

_____ ❷ **Which is *not* an effect of the tornado?**

Ⓐ dark, towering clouds

Ⓑ wind

Ⓒ hail

Ⓓ a flood

_____ ❸ **What caused the loud roaring sound?**

Ⓐ a tornado

Ⓑ a car

Ⓒ a train

Ⓓ a bus

_____ ❹ **"A roaring like a freight train passed over us."**

This is an example of _____

Ⓐ a train.

Ⓑ a metaphor.

Ⓒ a simile.

Ⓓ alliteration.

_____ ❺ **What will probably happen *next*?**

Ⓐ The narrator and Maria will have a picnic.

Ⓑ The narrator and Maria will get a ride home.

Ⓒ There will be a snowstorm.

Ⓓ The narrator and Maria will go swimming.

_____ ❻ **Why did Maria's mother look frightened?**

Ⓐ Her car would not start.

Ⓑ She was lost.

Ⓒ A big storm was coming.

Ⓓ She ran out of gas.

Word Power

Choose the English word from the Vocabulary list that correctly matches the definition.

very large in size; huge

_____

a tubelike form that is wide at the top and narrow at the bottom

_____

a loud noise

_____

to keep away from

_____

History of Clothes

Skill Overview

A heading is a word or phrase that introduces a section. It also describes and gives the main idea of the section. Headings help to organize the text and allow the reader to quickly see what the section will be about.

🎧 03

You look in your closet and say, "Mom, I don't have a thing to wear! Can we go shopping?" You may spend hours in the store choosing **garments**. You want to wear clothes that make you look and feel good. But where do all those clothes come from? Who made them, and how?

Jeans

If you're like most people, you have jeans. Levi Strauss invented them for gold miners in 1873. Today's jeans look much like the first ones. The pockets still have copper **rivets**. Strauss added them to make the pockets strong so that miners could carry gold.

Raincoats

If you own a raincoat, you can thank Charles Macintosh. He made the first **waterproof** cloth. He put a thin layer of rubber between two pieces of cloth. The cloth had a special liquid on it that helped the rubber stick to it. He made the cloth into raincoats. People loved them! They could stay dry when it rained.

Shoes

Years ago, **cobblers** made shoes for people when they ordered them. After they measured the person's foot, they chose the shoe form that matched. The cobblers used the form to cut leather uppers and soles. They **sewed** together the pieces of the uppers. Finally, they used tiny wooden **pegs** to attach the uppers and soles. All of this took days. Today, shoe pieces are mainly cut and put together on machines. Some shoes are **stitched,** and others are **glued**. This makes shoes cost less so that people can afford more pairs.

Vocabulary

garment
a piece of clothing

✪ **rivet**
a metal fastener used to hold two pieces of material together

waterproof
able to repel water

✪ **cobbler**
a person who mends or makes shoes

sew
to join two pieces of cloth together by putting thread through them with a needle

peg
a short pin or bolt

stitch
to fasten or join with a needle

glue
to fasten or join with a sticky substance

Reading Skill Comprehension Practice

 **Part 1**

Circle one of the headings below from the passage. Write the main idea or the section.

Jeans

Raincoats

Shoes

Main idea:

 **Part 2** Write one fact that you learned about each item below.

Jeans	Raincoats	Shoes
Today's jeans look like the first ones.	Raincoats prevent us from getting wet in the rain.	Cobblers are people who make shoes.

 **Part 3** Answer the questions below with complete sentences. Use the headings to help you locate the information.

Jeans	Raincoats
1. Why are there copper rivets on jeans?	**3.** Who made the first waterproof cloth?

	Shoes
2. When were jeans invented?	**4.** What is a person who makes shoes called?

14

Comprehension Review

Fill in the best answer for each question.

_____ **1** The *first* heading tells you that the section is about _____
- Ⓐ pants.
- Ⓑ skirts.
- Ⓒ raincoats.
- Ⓓ shoes.

_____ **2** You can learn about how people stay dry under the _____ heading.
- Ⓐ History of Clothes
- Ⓑ Shoes
- Ⓒ Raincoats
- Ⓓ Jeans

_____ **3** What information is *not* found under the *Shoes* heading?
- Ⓐ what cobblers did
- Ⓑ what Charles Macintosh invented
- Ⓒ how leather uppers were attached to soles
- Ⓓ how shoes are made today

_____ **4** Which happened *first*?
- Ⓐ Finally, they used tiny wooden pegs to attach the uppers and soles.
- Ⓑ They sewed together the pieces of the uppers.
- Ⓒ The cobblers used the form to cut leather uppers and soles.
- Ⓓ After they measured the person's foot, they chose the shoe form that matched.

_____ **5** If you didn't know what *garments* means, what could you do?
- Ⓐ Write the word.
- Ⓑ Spell the word.
- Ⓒ Read the paragraph again.
- Ⓓ Say the word.

_____ **6** Why is Charles Macintosh famous?
- Ⓐ He made the first waterproof cloth.
- Ⓑ He was a cobbler.
- Ⓒ He invented jeans.
- Ⓓ He was a gold miner.

Word Power

Choose the English word from the Vocabulary list that correctly matches the definition.

 a metal fastener used to hold two pieces of material together

_____

 a piece of clothing

_____

 able to repel water

_____

 a person who mends or makes shoes.

_____

15

SIGHT

Skill Overview

The main idea is the point that an author wishes to make about a topic—the central thought or message that the reader needs to understand. Readers must be able to identify the main idea and the supporting details or facts that support the main idea of a text.

Sight helps you see things in the world around you. Your eyes send **messages** to your brain, and your brain tells you what you are seeing. Eyesight is one of the most important ways people get along in the world. Have you ever worn a **blindfold**? If so, then you know how challenging life without sight can be.

The eye is an amazing **structure**. The white part of the eye is called the *sclera*. This is a **coating** that **covers** most of the eyeball. The *cornea* is part of the sclera. This part is clear and covers the colored part of the eye. The cornea is like a window that lets light

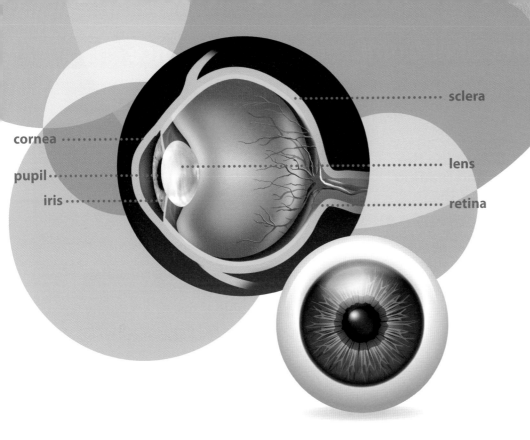

cornea
pupil
iris
sclera
lens
retina

into the eyeball. The iris and pupil are behind the cornea. The *iris* is the part that has color. The *pupil* is the black circle you see in the center of the iris. The iris **controls** the amount of light that comes through the pupil. When it is dark, the iris makes the pupil bigger to let in more light. When there is bright light, the iris makes the pupil smaller to let in less light.

Light that enters the eye then **reaches** the *lens*. The lens focuses the image onto the back of the eyeball, called the *retina*. The retina sends a message to the brain, and the brain tells you what you are seeing.

eyebrow

eyelid

eyelashes

eyelashes

Vocabulary

message
a short piece of information

✪ **blindfold**
a strip of cloth that covers someone's eyes and stops them from seeing

structure
an arrangement; something constructed or formed

✪ **coating**
a covering

cover
to put or spread something over something

control
to make something or someone else do something

reach
to arrive at

focus
to concentrate on a central point

Reading Skill Comprehension Practice

Part 1

There are several ways to determine the main idea. After listening to and reading the passage, tell what you think the main idea is.

1. Human eyes is an amazing structure with different parts.

2. _____

_____

Part 2 After rereading the passage, please fill in the web below with four supporting details for the main idea that you identified in Part 1.

1. Supporting Detail

_____

_____

2. Supporting Detail

_____

_____

Main Idea

Human eyes is an amazing structure with different parts.

_____

_____

3. Supporting Detail

_____

_____

4. Supporting Detail

_____

_____

Comprehension Review

Fill in the best answer for each question.

_____ ❶ **Which would be another good title for this passage?**

Ⓐ The Brain

Ⓑ Our Eyes and How We See

Ⓒ The Iris and the Pupil

Ⓓ How the Retina Works

_____ ❷ **The second paragraph is** *mostly* **about** _____

Ⓐ why we need to see.

Ⓑ the brain.

Ⓒ the parts of the eye.

Ⓓ how animals see.

_____ ❸ **Which is** *not* **a main idea?**

Ⓐ The white part of the eye is called the *sclera*.

Ⓑ Sight helps you see things in the world around you.

Ⓒ The eye is an amazing structure.

Ⓓ Your eyes send messages to your brain, and your brain tells you what you are seeing.

_____ ❹ **Which statement is true?**

Ⓐ The white part of the eye is called the *retina*.

Ⓑ The *retina* tells you what you are seeing.

Ⓒ The lens focuses the image on the *sclera*.

Ⓓ The iris controls the amount of light that comes through the pupil.

_____ ❺ **What causes the pupil to get bigger to let in more light?**

Ⓐ the sclera

Ⓑ the iris

Ⓒ the retina

Ⓓ the lens

_____ ❻ **How is the cornea** *"like a window"*?

Ⓐ It lets in light.

Ⓑ It is square.

Ⓒ It cannot open.

Ⓓ It is made of glass.

Word Power

Choose the English word from the Vocabulary list that correctly matches the definition.

 a covering

_____

 a short piece of information

_____

 to make something or someone else do something

_____

 an arrangement; something constructed or formed

_____

Reading Tip

 Compare means to describe how two things are the same, and **contrast** means to tell how they are different.

 Follow the instructions in Part 1 before listening to the CD and reading along with the passage.

Skill Overview

Authors use a compare-and-contrast structural pattern to show similarities and differences between topics, events, or people. Readers may recognize this pattern by the use of certain signal words such as *like*, *but*, *also*, and *no*.

▼ A manual stopwatch

Timing Races

 05

It is important to know who wins a race. **Athletes** can earn money if they win races. They can earn even more if they **break** a world **record**!

Long ago, **manual** stopwatches were used to time races. But they could only **measure** down to half a second. Today, **digital** timers are used to time races. Races are timed down to 0.001 of a second.

The 1932 Olympics were special. **Automatic** stopwatches were used for the first time. But they could only measure down to 0.10 of a second. In 1932, the winner of the men's 100-meter race finished in 10.30 seconds. The athlete who ran third finished in 10.40 seconds. One tenth (0.10) of a second is a long time in such a fast race! These days, a starter gun sets off a digital timer. This is much more exact.

Today's timers can measure down to 0.001 (one thousandth) of a second! The starting blocks have speakers.

▲ A sprint starter

Runners hear the starter gun through the speakers. They all hear it at the same time. Runners take off when they hear this sound. A runner may **take off** before the sound. This is called a *false start*. All runners are given a warning after a false start. The next runner who makes a false start is disqualified from the race. This means the runner is taken out of the race.

The finish line at the 2004 Olympics had a laser beam across it. Runners "broke" the beam when they crossed the line, stopping the timer. This is a very **accurate** way to time races.

▲ A starter gun

▼ A laser beam

▼ A digital timer

21

Reading Skill Comprehension Practice

same
different
like
unlike

both
have in common
but
differ

while
similar
as well as
yet

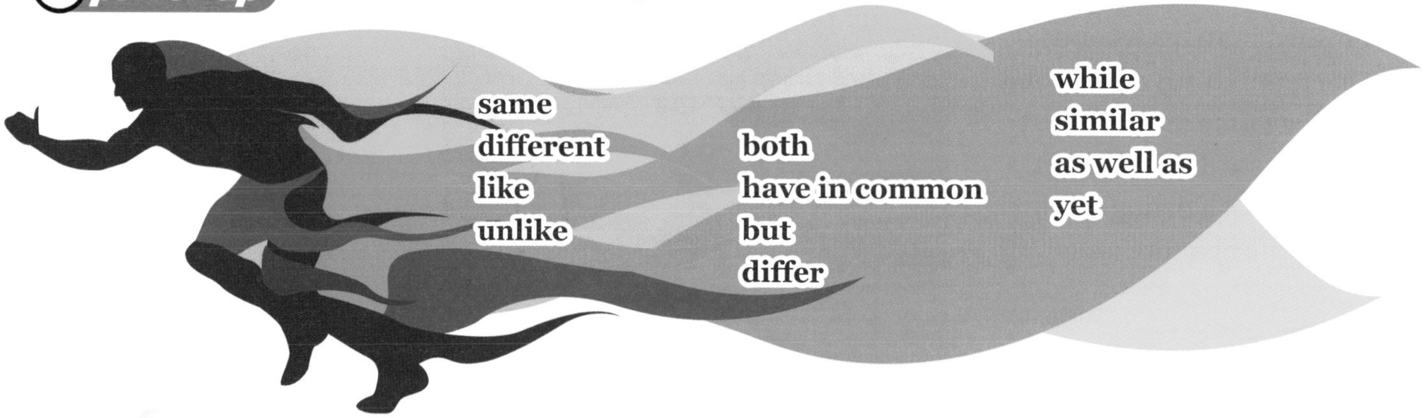

Part 1

Please compare two items in the classroom (for example, a pen and a pencil) and fill in the diagram.

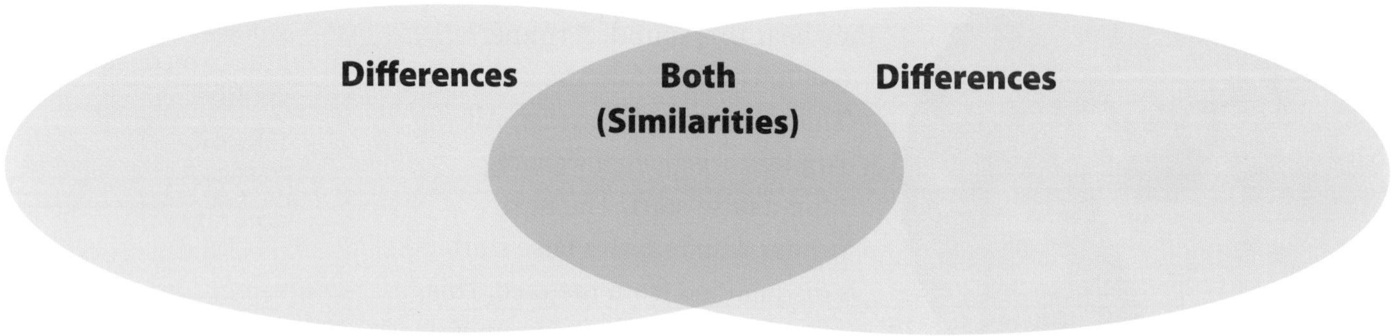

> [....]   [....]

Differences   **Both (Similarities)**   **Differences**

Part 2

Use the T-chart below to compare and contrast manual stopwatches with digital timers.

Manual Stopwatches vs. Digital Timers

● Similarities	● Differences
Manual stopwatches and digital timers are both used for timing races.	Digital timers are more accurate than manual timers.

Part 3

Write one sentence telling how manual stopwatches and digital timers are the same. Then write one sentence with signal words telling how they are different.

Same: _____

Different: _____

Comprehension Review

Fill in the best answer for each question.

_____ ❶ Unlike today's races, races long ago were _____
- Ⓐ timed with a digital timer.
- Ⓑ longer.
- Ⓒ fast.
- Ⓓ timed with a manual stopwatch.

_____ ❷ Both manual stopwatches and digital timers _____
- Ⓐ are stopped with laser beams.
- Ⓑ can measure to 0.001 of a second.
- Ⓒ have been used in races.
- Ⓓ can only measure to 0.50 of a second.

_____ ❸ Unlike the 1932 Olympics, the 2004 Olympics had _____
- Ⓐ a laser beam across the finish line.
- Ⓑ races.
- Ⓒ winners.
- Ⓓ many athletes.

_____ ❹ "The next runner who makes a false start is disqualified from the race."
If you did not know what _disqualified_ means, what could you do?
- Ⓐ Look at the title.
- Ⓑ Write the word.
- Ⓒ Read the next sentence.
- Ⓓ Say the word out loud.

_____ ❺ Which happened _last_?
- Ⓐ Manual stopwatches were used.
- Ⓑ A laser beam was used at the finish line.
- Ⓒ The first automatic stopwatch was used.
- Ⓓ The winner of the men's 100-meter race finished in 10.30 seconds.

_____ ❻ The author wrote this passage to _____
- Ⓐ get you to run in a race.
- Ⓑ teach you how to run safely.
- Ⓒ tell the story of a great athlete.
- Ⓓ tell how races are timed.

Word Power

Choose the English word from the Vocabulary list that correctly matches the definition.

 1. precise and correct

_____

 2. by hand; requiring physical skill

_____

 3. a person who is very good at sports or physical exercise

_____

 4. using computer technology processed by computers

_____

23

ZOOS
Old and New

35

▲ An old-fashioned zoo back in 1910

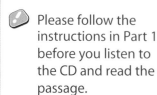
Skill Overview

The topic is the subject of a text or the general category to which the ideas in the passage belong. It can often be stated in a word or a phrase. The topic can help the reader make predictions about the text.

 06

Early Chinese rulers kept private collections of animals. But the first zoo we know of was in Egypt around 1500 B.C. It was Queen Hatshepsut's zoo. She received **wild** animals as gifts. They were given to her as a tribute by peoples that her army had conquered.

Before modern zoos, there were small collections of animals called *menageries*. In most menageries, animals were kept in small, dirty

24

cages. Modern zoos came about as a reaction to this. In modern zoos, animals are kept in areas that look like natural **habitats**. This change did not take place all at once. For many years, the largest and most **modern** zoos kept animals in cages. Some zoos still keep animals caged. Often, newspapers write articles about this. They speak out against zoos for the way the animals are treated.

Long ago, the purpose of zoos was to let people see **rare** animals from distant places that most people could never visit. But now there are many other reasons for keeping animals in zoos. For example, many animal **species** have become **endangered**. This means that it is harder to find them in their native habitats. Some animals are no longer found in the wild at all. They exist only in confined places. Sometimes zoologists are able to breed the **captive** animals. They also try to help return the species to its native habitat. Sadly, they are not always able to do this. Often, this is because the habitat no longer exists due to changes in land use.

At one time, hunters captured and sold animals to zoos that needed them. This still occurs today. But now, zoos often sell or trade their animals to other zoos. Also, many countries now have laws that limit the capture of wild animals. So, the animals you see in the zoo may never have lived in the wild. Instead, they were born and raised in captivity.

People concerned with animal rights don't like the display of animals in zoos. But other people feel that zoos care for and protect the animals. They feel that this is why many exotic species are still alive today.

Vocabulary

wild
living in nature without human care; not tame

cage
a space surrounded on all sides by bars or wire

habitat
the place or environment where a plant or animal naturally or normally lives and grows

modern
new, up-to-date

rare
not common; very unusual

species
a set of animals or plants in which the members have similar characteristics

endangered
describing an animal or plant that soon may not exist

captive
captured and held in a place

▼ Animals are born and raised in zoos nowadays.

▼ A menagerie

▲ An endangered white tiger in a modern zoo.

Reading Skill Comprehension Practice

 **Part 1** The topic of this passage is zoos. Write the information you think you will learn from reading a passage about this topic. After responding, please listen to the CD as you read the first two paragraphs.

I think I will learn about _____

_____

 **Part 2** Now that you have read the first two paragraphs, your prediction about the content of the passage may have changed. Write your new prediction about the rest of the passage. After responding, please listen to the CD and read the rest of the paragraphs.

I think the rest of the passage will be about _____

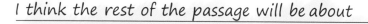

_____

 **Part 3** Making predictions can help you better understand what you read. Now please refer back to the passage and write a short summary of what you have learned about zoos.

_____

_____

_____

_____

_____

_____

Comprehension Review

Fill in the best answer for each question.

_____ ❶ **This passage is about zoos. What will you probably *not* learn about?**

Ⓐ what early zoos were like

Ⓑ how zoos have changed over time

Ⓒ animals in the wild

Ⓓ zoos and animal rights

_____ ❷ **People who like _____will probably like this passage.**

Ⓐ sports

Ⓑ math

Ⓒ music

Ⓓ animals

_____ ❸ **You will probably read about _____**

Ⓐ why animals are put in zoos.

Ⓑ how to become a zoologist.

Ⓒ animal habitats.

Ⓓ wild animals.

_____ ❹ **"For example, many animal species have become endangered."**

If you didn't know the meaning of *endangered*, what could you do?

Ⓐ Read the title.

Ⓑ Write the word.

Ⓒ Read the rest of the paragraph.

Ⓓ Read the sentence again.

_____ ❺ ***Before* modern zoos, animals were _____**

Ⓐ endangered.

Ⓑ kept in small, dirty cages.

Ⓒ protected.

Ⓓ living in one place.

_____ ❻ **Which statement is false?**

Ⓐ Hunters no longer capture and sell animals to zoos.

Ⓑ Early Chinese rulers kept private collections of animals.

Ⓒ Many animals have become endangered.

Ⓓ None of zoos keep animals caged.

Word Power

Choose the English word from the Vocabulary list that correctly matches the definition.

new, up-to-date

_____

describing an animal or plant that soon may not exist

_____

captured and held in a place

_____

not common; very unusual

_____

LESSON 07
Character

Think about who the **main character** is and who the supporting characters are in the story.

A **character's physical characteristics** describe how he or she looks.

The **personality traits of a character** describe what kind of person he or she is. These traits can also be determined by the character's actions and speech.

Mrs. Gerson's Home Run

Skill Overview

Characters are the people that a story is about. There are main characters and supporting characters. The development of the characters provides the reader with an understanding of how stories work. The development of the characters includes actions, physical descriptions, and character descriptions.

🎧 07

It all started when Big Mike hit a home run into Mrs. Gerson's front yard. The next thing the boys knew, Mrs. Gerson herself was **ambling** onto the field. She carried the baseball like it was a rotten egg.

"You boys!" she said. "I told you not to hit the ball into my yard!"

© MCININCH / DREAMSTIME.COM

▼ A baseball diamond

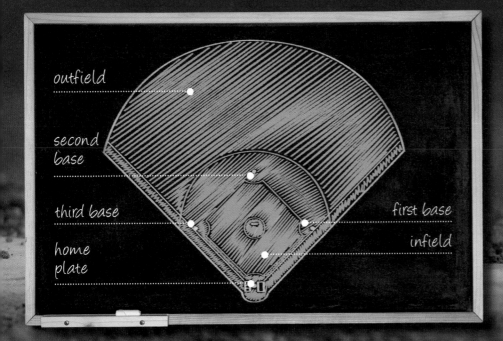

outfield

second base

third base

home plate

first base

infield

Vocabulary

⭐ **amble**
to walk slowly

determined
set on doing something

bat
a specially shaped piece of wood used for hitting the ball in many games

swing
a curved movement made with the arms and legs

approach
to come toward

pretend
to behave as if something is true when you know it is not

⭐ **trudge**
to walk slowly with a lot of effort

cross
to go from one side to another

"We're sorry, Mrs. Gerson," Nick said. "Could we have it back?"

"Yeah, you can have it back," she said. "If you let me hit a home run." **Determined**, she marched to home plate and picked up a **bat**.

The kids didn't know what to do. Mrs. Gerson stood with her feet on home plate and waved the bat around over her head. Kevin took the ball to the pitcher's mound. Then he tossed it toward home as gently as he could. Mrs. Gerson took a wild **swing** and somehow caught a piece of it.

"Run!" the boys shouted all at once.

So she started running toward first base. Tommy walked out from behind the plate and picked up the ball. Mrs. Gerson wasn't even halfway toward first, so Tommy threw the ball over the first baseman's head. Nick walked as slowly as he could to get it while Mrs. Gerson **approached** first base.

"That way!" Mike pointed toward second. Nick threw the ball into some bushes. Kevin and Andy **pretended** to look for it while Mrs. Gerson **trudged** around second, around third, and then headed home. Finally, Kevin picked up the ball and threw it into the bleachers. Mrs. Gerson **crossed** home plate and raised her arms in victory. Everyone cheered.

"Thank you," Mrs. Gerson said. She started walking back to her house. The she turned around. "You boys better get to work," she said. "You need a lot of practice."

29

Reading Skill Comprehension Practice

Physical characteristics describe features of a person's body, such as . . .

- curly hair
- pimples
- crooked nose
- skinny
- chubby
- dark skin

Personality traits are words used to describe how a character acts or feels, such as . . .

- arrogant
- loyal
- selfish
- helpful
- kind
- greedy

Think about how you pictured Mrs. Gerson when you were listening to and reading the story. Write two or three sentences describing Mrs. Gerson's <u>physical characteristics</u>.

I imagine Mrs. Gerson as an old grandmother because of how the author describes the way she walks.

Write one or two sentences describing Mrs. Gerson's <u>personality traits</u>, or what type of person she is.

I think Mrs. Gerson is brave and ambitious. She is not afraid of trying new things even at her age — not to mention that she asked to hit a homerun!

Write your favorite personality trait of Mrs. Gerson. Then list some of the behaviors, actions, and words from the passage show that this is one of her traits.

Trait: _____

How it is shown in the passage: _____

Comprehension Review

Fill in the best answer for each question.

_____ **❶ Mrs. Gerson is _____ baseball.**
Ⓐ good at
Ⓑ sorry about
Ⓒ afraid of
Ⓓ curious about

_____ **❷ Mrs. Gerson is probably _not_**
_____
Ⓐ a neighbor.
Ⓑ a mean person.
Ⓒ older than the boys.
Ⓓ happy about hitting a home run.

_____ **❸ Which sentence is probably true?**
Ⓐ Mrs. Gerson is very athletic.
Ⓑ Mrs. Gerson plays baseball a lot.
Ⓒ Mrs. Gerson is not very good at baseball.
Ⓓ Mrs. Gerson is very angry at the boys.

_____ **❹ You can guess that _____**
Ⓐ the ball has gone into Mrs. Gerson's yard before.
Ⓑ Mrs. Gerson will call the police.
Ⓒ the boys are really afraid of Mrs. Gerson.
Ⓓ Mrs. Gerson is good at sports.

_____ **❺ Why did the boys play so badly?**
Ⓐ Mrs. Gerson asked them to play badly.
Ⓑ They did not know how to play baseball.
Ⓒ They wanted Mrs. Gerson to hit a home run.
Ⓓ They did not practice that day.

_____ **❻ _"The next thing the boys knew, Mrs. Gerson herself was ambling onto the field."_**
What does _ambling_ mean in this sentence?
Ⓐ swimming
Ⓑ driving
Ⓒ dancing
Ⓓ walking

Word Power

Choose the English word from the Vocabulary list that correctly matches the definition.

 to come toward

_____

 set on doing something

_____

 to walk slowly

_____

 to behave as if something is true when you know it is not

_____

Reading Tip

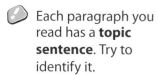

- Each paragraph you read has a **topic sentence**. Try to identify it.

- The **main idea** is located in the topic sentence. The main idea is the most important concept that the author wants you to understand.

Earth's Cycle of Seasons

Skill Overview

A **topic sentence** is a general statement that expresses the main idea of a paragraph. It is usually the first sentence in a paragraph and is followed by sentences that support it. The topic sentence prepares the reader for what to expect in the rest of the paragraph.

▼ Cycle of seasons

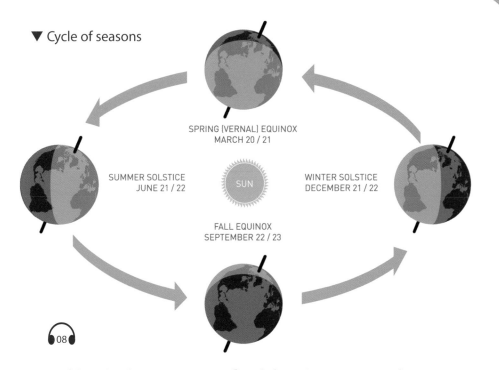

SPRING (VERNAL) EQUINOX
MARCH 20 / 21

SUMMER SOLSTICE
JUNE 21 / 22

SUN

WINTER SOLSTICE
DECEMBER 21 / 22

FALL EQUINOX
SEPTEMBER 22 / 23

🎧 08

Earth's spinning causes a **cycle** of changing seasons. There are four seasons each year: spring, summer, autumn, and winter. The seasons are not the same everywhere at the same time. They are different because of Earth's **rotations** and **revolutions**.

Here's how it works:

Earth **rotates** one time each day. But Earth's **axis** is not straight up and down. It **tilts** a little. So, Earth tilts a little, too.

Earth **orbits**, or circles, the sun one time each year. This is one revolution.

Because Earth is tilted, the sun's most direct **rays** hit Earth at different places. This depends on Earth's rotations and revolutions. Some places experience daylight while other places experience nighttime. This is a result of Earth's rotations and revolutions.

Vocabulary

cycle
a period of time that repeats itself regularly and in the same order

rotation
movement in a circle around a fixed point

✪ **revolution**
a circular movement around something

rotate
to turn in a circle around a fixed point

✪ **axis**
the center around which something rotates

tilt
to move or cause to move into a sloping position

orbit
to move around a second object or point

ray
a narrow beam of light, heat, etc., traveling in a straight line

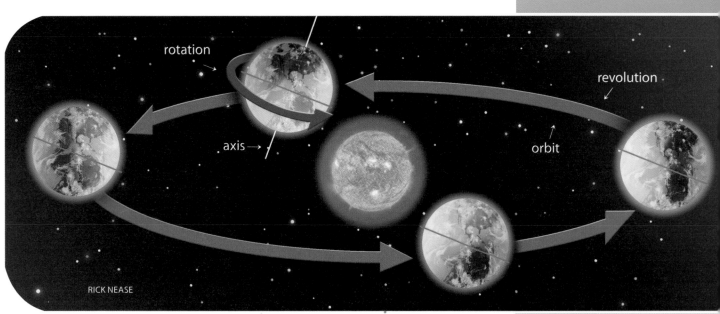

rotation

revolution

axis →

orbit

RICK NEASE

Reading Skill Comprehension Practice

Part 1 Write the topic sentence of the first paragraph.

_____

Part 2

Please identify the topic sentence among these three sentences. Put a T in front of the topic sentence.
Then put the sentences in order.

_____ Earth is the third planet from the sun.

_____ Earth is a planet.

_____ Earth is the only planet known to have life on it.

1. _____

2. _____

3. _____

Part 3 Read each pair of sentences. Choose the one that is the topic sentence.

1
A. Starfish make their home in tide pools.
B. Many animals and plants live in tide pools.

2
A. Animals that live in the desert adapt in many ways.
B. Many animals are nocturnal—they sleep during the day when it is very hot.

3
A. Blue whales grow to be about 80 feet (24.4 m) long.
B. The blue whale is the largest animal in the sea.

Comprehension Review

Fill in the best answer for each question.

_____ ❶ *"Earth's spinning causes a cycle of changing seasons."*
Which of these provides details to support the topic sentence?
Ⓐ There are four seasons each year: spring, summer, autumn, and winter.
Ⓑ So, Earth tilts a little, too.
Ⓒ This is one revolution.
Ⓓ But Earth's axis is not straight up and down.

_____ ❷ **Which of these is *not* a topic sentence?**
Ⓐ Earth's spinning causes a cycle of changing seasons.
Ⓑ Earth orbits, or circles, the sun one time each year.
Ⓒ It tilts a little.
Ⓓ Earth rotates one time each day.

_____ ❸ **The topic sentences tell you that this passage is mostly about _____**
Ⓐ summer and winter.　Ⓒ life in the oceans.
Ⓑ how Earth moves.　Ⓓ our solar system.

_____ ❹ **What is the effect of Earth's spinning?**
Ⓐ Earth's tilt
Ⓑ sun's ray
Ⓒ oceans
Ⓓ changing seasons

_____ ❺ **What is another word for _orbits_?**
Ⓐ circles
Ⓑ seasons
Ⓒ swirls
Ⓓ runs

_____ ❻ **A _____ is one orbit, or circle, that Earth makes around the sun each year.**
Ⓐ tilt
Ⓑ revolution
Ⓒ rotation
Ⓓ season

Word Power

Choose the English word from the Vocabulary list that correctly matches the definition.

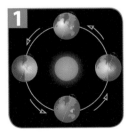 to move around a second object or point

_____

 the center around which something rotates

_____

 to move or cause to move into a sloping position

_____

 a period of time that repeats itself regularly and in the same order

_____

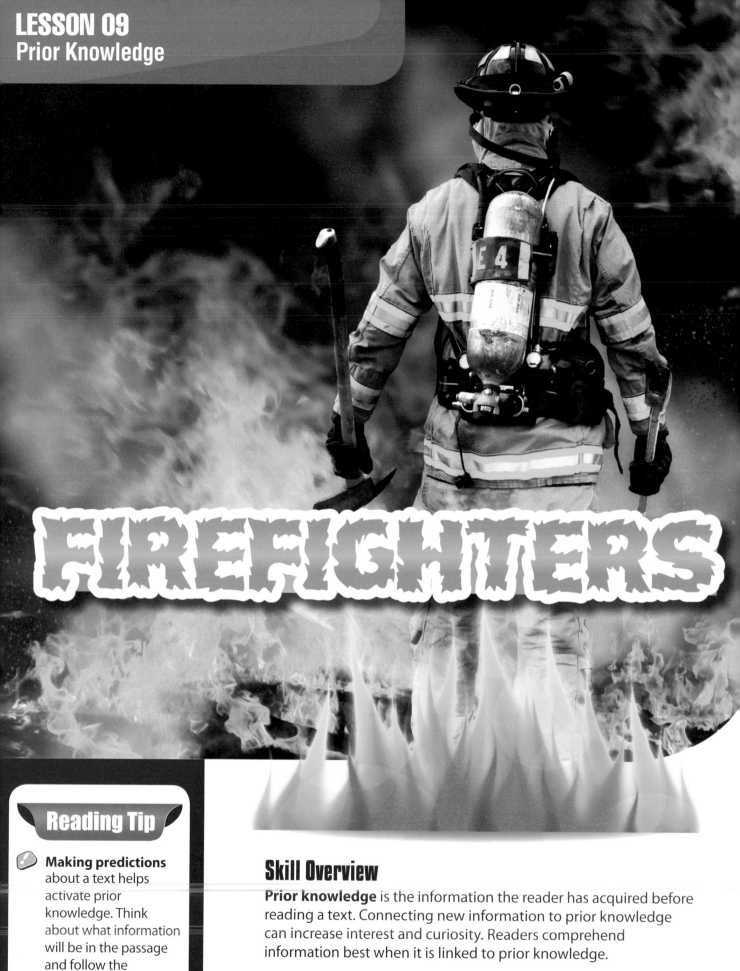

FIREFIGHTERS

Reading Tip

Making predictions about a text helps activate prior knowledge. Think about what information will be in the passage and follow the instructions in Part 1.

Skill Overview

Prior knowledge is the information the reader has acquired before reading a text. Connecting new information to prior knowledge can increase interest and curiosity. Readers comprehend information best when it is linked to prior knowledge.

Firefighters are very busy. They can be called to a fire at any time of the day or night. They must be ready at all times **in case of** an **emergency**. Some firefighters live at the fire station part of the time. They have beds, bathrooms, and a kitchen there. They also have rooms for relaxing. If there is no fire, they get to sleep at night. When they are at the station, they check the **equipment** and the fire trucks. They inspect the nozzles on the **hoses** to make sure they are working. They check the engine to be sure there is enough gas and oil, and they check the air in the tires.

There are many different emergencies besides fires. Sometimes firefighters are called to help people in medical emergencies. Sometimes they **rescue** people who are trapped or in danger. Other times, they clear areas near fires or other disasters. They help people after earthquakes, terrible storms, and crashes. They spend many hours working to prevent fires from starting, too.

Firefighters are almost always working, even if there are no fires. They go to schools to teach about fire **safety**. They study to be sure they are the best at their jobs. They practice putting out fires, too, so that they are ready when there is a fire. Firefighters also check fire safety in local businesses. They need to make sure businesses are safe for both the workers and the customers.

When they go back to the station, firefighters take turns making their meals and doing the **chores**. Sometimes firefighters give tours of the fire station. They show the equipment in the station and on the trucks. They might even show how the **sirens** work!

© 2009 Jupiterimages Corporation (/Photos.com)

Vocabulary

★ **in case of**
in the event of

emergency
an urgent problem

equipment
tools

hose
a long plastic or rubber pipe

nozzle

hose

rescue
to help someone or something out of a dangerous, harmful, or unpleasant situation

safety
the state of being safe from harm

chore
a job or piece of work that needs to be done regularly

★ **siren**
a device for making a loud warning noise

Reading Skill Comprehension Practice

 Making a **KWL** chart on a piece of paper will help you a lot with using prior knowledge.

K section
....
information you already know
▶ Think about what you already know about firefighters and write them on the chart.

W section
....
information you want to learn
▶ Make a list of questions you want to learn about firefighters.

L section
....
information you learned after reading the passage
▶ Fill in the information you learned from the passage.

Part 1 Write two predictions about this passage.

1. The passage will explain a firefighter's daily routine.

2. _____

3. _____

Part 2 Think about something you already know about firefighters. Then write two questions you have about firefighters.

1. How many hours does a firefighter usually work a day?

2. _____

3. _____

Part 3 Try to answer two questions from Part 2 with information you learned from the passage. If the information you need to answer the questions is not in the passage, please choose two other questions from the KWL chart that you can answer.

1. _____

_____

2. _____

_____

Comprehension Review

Fill in the best answer for each question.

_____ ① **You already know that fires are dangerous. This will help you learn about_____**
- Ⓐ chores.
- Ⓑ emergencies.
- Ⓒ fire safety.
- Ⓓ families.

_____ ② **Knowing what a fire station is helps you learn _____**
- Ⓐ what an engine is.
- Ⓑ what firefighters do at the station.
- Ⓒ where fires happen.
- Ⓓ how schools stay safe.

_____ ③ **Thinking about _____ helps you understand what nozzles, hoses, and sirens are.**
- Ⓐ earthquakes
- Ⓑ businesses
- Ⓒ schools
- Ⓓ fire trucks

_____ ④ **Which is _not_ a job that firefighters do?**
- Ⓐ build new fire stations
- Ⓑ teach about fire safety
- Ⓒ check the equipment to be sure it is working
- Ⓓ help when there is an emergency

_____ ⑤ **You would read this if you wanted to _____**
- Ⓐ learn how to stay safe.
- Ⓑ buy a fire truck.
- Ⓒ learn how to become a firefighter.
- Ⓓ learn what firefighters do.

_____ ⑥ **Which statement is _not_ true?**
- Ⓐ Some firefighters live at the station part of the time.
- Ⓑ Firefighters only put out fires.
- Ⓒ Firefighters give tours of the station.
- Ⓓ Firefighters work to prevent fires from starting.

Word Power

Choose the English word from the Vocabulary list that correctly matches the definition.

 tools

_____

 an urgent problem

_____

 the state of being safe from harm

_____

 a job or piece of work that needs to be done regularly

_____

LESSON 10

Reading Tip

- Think about what kinds of texts can be written in sequential order.

- Think about situations where it is very important to follow steps in sequential order.

A Simple Budget

Skill Overview

Sequential order is a text structure in which information is presented in an organized manner. Events and ideas are described in the order that they happened. Recognizing this structure can help readers better understand the text.

Let's look at a simple budget. Sam gets an **allowance** of $5.00 per week. She also earns $15.50 per week helping her neighbor Ms. Liu in the garden. Both amounts are her **income**. Sam's expenses include $9.50 per week for a movie ticket and $5.00 per week for eating out. At the end of each week, Sam has $6.00 left after her expenses. She puts this $6.00 in her savings. So, how do you make a **budget**?

Sam's Weekly Budget

Income

Allowance	$5.00
Helping neighbor	$15.50
Total income	**$20.50**

Expenses

Movie ticket	$9.50
Eating out	$5.00
Total expenses	**$14.50**

Total income − total expenses = $6.00 savings

The first step is to **keep track of** your income and **expenses**, just like Sam did. Start by writing down in a notebook what you earn and spend. Do this for a few weeks. This helps you keep track of your money each week.

Next, you need to **plan** ahead. What do you need to save for? Once you know, you can plan for the weeks ahead. Under the heading *Income*, make a list of what you will earn. This might include your allowance or money from extra chores at home. Now, make a list under the heading *Expenses*. Write down what you think you will spend your money on. This might include food, movies, CDs—it's up to you!

The information in your notebook will help you work it all out. Now, **add up** all the things in your Income list. This will be your total income. Then add up all the things in your Expenses list to get your total expenses. Next, **subtract** the total expenses from the total income. This will tell you how much money you'll have left at the end of the week. This money can go into your savings.

Vocabulary

allowance
an amount of money given regularly (often in exchange for work done)

income
money that is earned

budget
the amount of money you have available to spend

★ **keep track of**
to make certain that you know what is happening or has happened

expense
money that is spent

plan
a set of decisions about how to do something in the future

★ **add up**
to calculate the total value

subtract
to take away a number or amount

41

Reading Skill Comprehension Practice

power up Many passages that are written in sequential order contain key sequence words:

- ✔ First
- ✔ First of all
- ✔ To begin
- ✔ Second, Third, . . .
- ✔ Then
- ✔ After that
- ✔ Last
- ✔ Lastly
- ✔ Finally

Part 1 Identify the signal words for sequential order in the passage.

- The first step
- _____
- _____

Part 2 The passage describes the important steps for creating a budget. Write five important steps below in sequential order.

Step 1 _____

Step 2 _____

Step 3 _____

Step 4 _____

Step 5 _____

Part 3 Write a short paragraph that describes how to make a budget. Use the key words in Part 1 and the steps in Part 2 to help you.

_____

_____

_____

Comprehension Review

Fill in the best answer for each question.

① Which is the _first_ step in making a budget?

Ⓐ Write down what you earn and spend in a notebook.

Ⓑ Make a list under the heading *Expenses*.

Ⓒ Next, you need to plan ahead.

Ⓓ Now, add up all the things in your Income list.

② _After_ you make a list of what you will earn, you should _____

Ⓐ spend all your money.

Ⓑ keep track of your money each week.

Ⓒ write down what you earn and spend in a notebook.

Ⓓ make a list under the heading *Expenses*.

③ Which is the _last_ step in making a budget?

Ⓐ Plan ahead.

Ⓑ Subtract the total expenses from the total income.

Ⓒ Make a list under the heading *Expenses*.

Ⓓ Make a list of what you will earn.

④ Why is it important to make a budget?

Ⓐ It can help you plan your savings.

Ⓑ It can help you spend more money.

Ⓒ It can help you earn money.

Ⓓ It can help you make more money.

⑤ Which word means "_money you earn_"?

Ⓐ income

Ⓑ expenses

Ⓒ budget

Ⓓ spending

⑥ The author wants you to _____

Ⓐ buy a CD.

Ⓑ stop spending money.

Ⓒ make a budget.

Ⓓ go to the movies.

Word Power

Choose the English word from the Vocabulary list that correctly matches the definition.

 an amount of money given regularly

_____

 money that is earned

_____

 money that is spent

_____

 to take away a number or amount

_____

LESSON 11
Meaning Clues to Predict

Reading Tip

Use the **title, photos, and headings** to make predictions about the passage and then answer the question in Part 1.

Meaning clues can help you make predictions about the content, action, and events in a text.

STATES OF MATTER

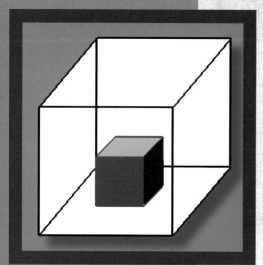

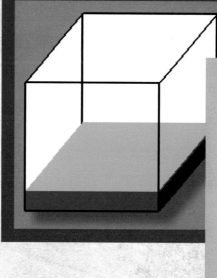

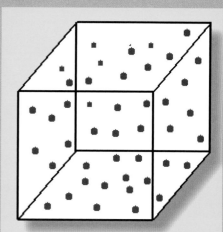

Vocabulary

state
condition of being

exist
to have real being, whether material or spiritual

Skill Overview

Meaning clues such as titles, headings, photos, and text layout can help readers comprehend what they read. By looking closely at the surrounding words and sentences, clues and hints can be discovered that help readers understand the main idea of the text.

 11

There are three **states** of matter: solid, liquid, and gas. All matter can **exist** in any and all of these states.

44

SOLID

When water is a solid, you can skate on it. You can put it in your drinks to make them cold—we call this ice.

LIQUID

When water is a liquid, you can swim in it, drink it, take a shower in it, or water plants with it. You can fill your fishbowl with it.

GAS

When water is a gas, it is called water **vapor** or **steam**; it is the stuff that clouds are made of. Water vapor would never stay in your dog's bowl. You see it as steam **rising** from a kettle or a cup of hot coffee.

Substances can change from one state of matter to another at different temperatures. For example, they may **melt** or **evaporate**. However, changing the states won't change the molecules. They stay the same. Water molecules are the same whether they are ice, water, or vapor.

Vocabulary

vapor
gas or extremely small drops of moisture that result from the heating of a liquid

steam
the hot gas that is produced when water boils

rise
to move from a lower position to a higher one

substance
any types of solids, gas or liquids

melt
to turn from something solid into something soft or liquid

⭐**evaporate**
to change from a liquid to a gas, especially by heating

Reading Skill Comprehension Practice

 **Part 1** Think about how different parts of the pages can help you make predictions about the passage. What can you predict from the title, the photos, and the headings in this passage?

- **Title** — The passage will be about _____
- **Photos** — Judging from the photos, _____
- **Headings** — The passage will describe _____

Part 2 Think about the predictions you made in Part 1. Then answer the questions below.

(YES) (NO) Were your predictions about the passage correct?

Please explain why your predictions about the passage were correct or incorrect.

_____
_____

What clues helped you make your predictions? ☐ Title ☐ Photos ☐ Headings

How did they help you make predictions about the passage?

_____
_____

Part 3 Explain how making predictions helps you as a reader.

Making predictions helps me _____
_____

Comprehension Review

Fill in the best answer for each question.

_____ ❶ *"When water is a solid, you can skate on it."*
The word _solid_ is a clue that you will read about _____
- Ⓐ drinking.
- Ⓑ ice.
- Ⓒ steam.
- Ⓓ a river.

_____ ❷ *"There are three states of matter: solid, liquid, and gas."*
Which word tells you that you will read about the water you drink?
- Ⓐ liquid
- Ⓑ gas
- Ⓒ solid
- Ⓓ matter

_____ ❸ **This passage tells you about solids, liquids, and gases. The passage could be part of _____**
- Ⓐ a history book.
- Ⓑ a math book.
- Ⓒ a science book.
- Ⓓ a book of poetry.

_____ ❹ *"Liquid"*
Which does *not* fit under this heading?
- Ⓐ drinking water
- Ⓑ water for swimming
- Ⓒ water for plants
- Ⓓ water vapor

_____ ❺ **What are clouds made of?**
- Ⓐ water vapor
- Ⓑ liquid
- Ⓒ ice
- Ⓓ hot coffee

_____ ❻ **Which one is true?**
- Ⓐ Water cannot change its state.
- Ⓑ Matter can be a solid, a liquid, or a gas.
- Ⓒ Molecules change when their state changes.
- Ⓓ Clouds are made of solid matter.

Word Power

Choose the English word from the Vocabulary list that correctly matches the definition.

1 to change from a liquid to a gas, especially by heating

_____

2 condition of being

_____

3 any types of solids, gas or liquids

_____

4 to turn from something solid into something soft or liquid

_____

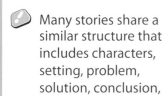

Reading Tip

Many stories share a similar structure that includes characters, setting, problem, solution, conclusion, and author's message.

The **main character** is the central figure of a story. Think about who the main character is in this passage. What are her actions and behaviors?

Vocabulary

✪**pick on somebody**
to repeatedly single someone out for criticism or unkind treatment

✪**tear up**
to pull or be pulled apart, or to pull pieces off

tease
to laugh at someone or say unkind things about him or her

ashamed
embarrassed

Skill Overview

The plot of a story may include a main problem and a solution. The problem, often introduced at the beginning of the story, is a key part of the plot, or action, of the story. Authors usually put the solution at the end of the story.

TIA AND THE BULLY

🎧 12

Tia was 11 but very small for her age. Everyone in her family was tall. Tia wished someday soon she would be tall, too.

One of the girls at Tia's school liked to **pick on** her. She would take food from Tia's lunch and eat it. She would break Tia's pencils and **tear up** her lessons. She would get other kids to **tease** Tia, too. Tia never told the teacher or her parents about the bully. She was too **ashamed**.

That summer, Tia grew and grew. When she went back to school, she was the tallest girl in her class. She was even taller than the **bully**. She could have taken the bully's lunch and eaten it. She could have broken her pencils and torn up her lessons. But Tia didn't do any of those things. When her friends asked her why, she **simply** replied, "Because even though I'm bigger than she is now, I don't ever want to be a bully."

Over time, the bully felt bad about what she had done. She asked Tia to **forgive** her. Soon, the girls became good friends.

One day, a new girl came into class. She didn't like Tia's friend and soon began to bully her. She did the same things that the bully had done to Tia. Tia could have let her do those things to her new friend. She could have thought, "Let her see how it feels to be bullied like she did to me." **Instead**, Tia told the new girl to stop picking on her friend. The new girl was afraid of Tia, so she stopped what she was doing.

When Tia's friend found out what she had done for her, she felt happy to have a friend like Tia. And Tia was happy to be a friend instead of a bully.

Vocabulary

simply
only

bully
a person who teases, hurts, or threatens others

forgive
to pardon, or accept, a wrong action done by someone else

instead
as an alternative or substitute

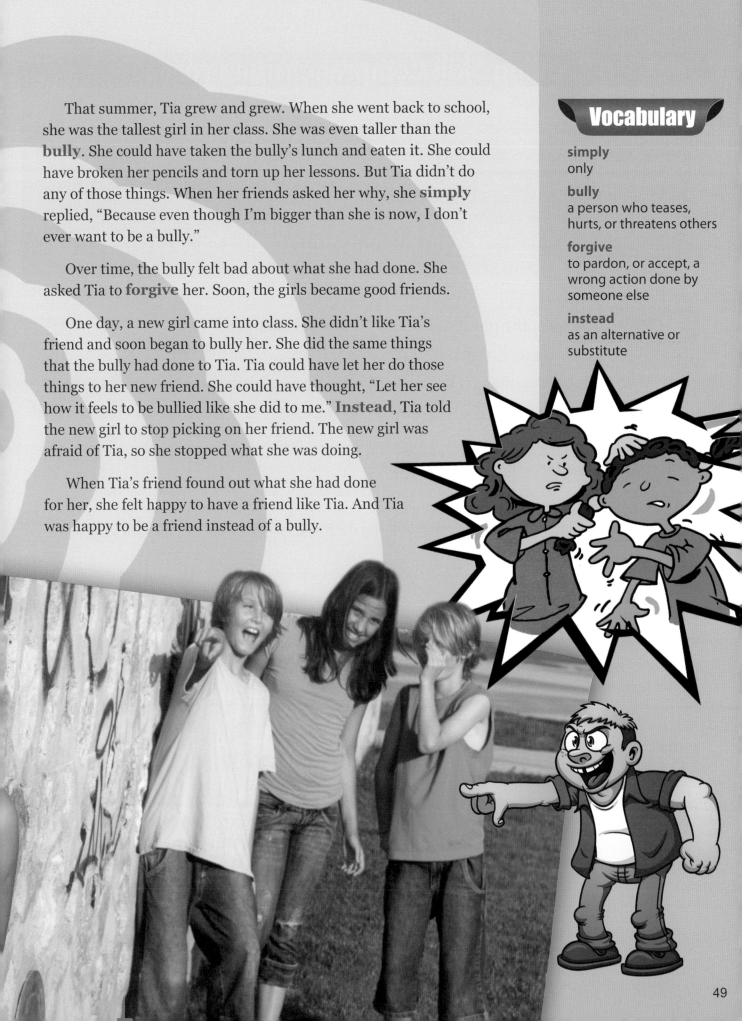

Reading Skill Comprehension Practice

The **setting of a story** tells when and where the story takes place.

⇒ Some stories have specific settings, while others take place at an indefinite time or place.

The plot of the story tells what happened.

⇒ It usually includes a problem the main character must solve, the steps the character takes to solve it, the solution to the problem, and the ending of the story.

 **Answer the questions about Tia's behavior and actions.**

1. What did Tia do when the bully bullied her? Did she tell her parents or her teacher? Did she fight back?

_____

2. Did Tia bully anyone else? Why or why not?

_____

3. How did Tia get the new bully to stop bullying her friend? What did she tell the new bully?

_____

 **Describe the setting.**

The setting is _____

 Write a problem and a solution from the story.

Problem	Solution

Comprehension Review

Fill in the best answer for each question.

_____ ❶ **Which is _not_ a problem for Tia?**
- Ⓐ She was very small for her age.
- Ⓑ She was picked on by a girl at school.
- Ⓒ She was happy to be a friend instead of a bully.
- Ⓓ She was too ashamed to ask for help.

_____ ❷ **The second paragraph tells you this story is _mostly_ about _____**
- Ⓐ how Tia learned to cook.
- Ⓑ Tia's problem with math.
- Ⓒ Tia's problem with her mother and father.
- Ⓓ Tia's problem with a bully.

_____ ❸ **This story tells about _____**
- Ⓐ a problem and how it was solved.
- Ⓑ how to do something.
- Ⓒ a legend.
- Ⓓ how two things are the same and how they are different.

_____ ❹ **Why didn't Tia tell her parents about the bully?**
- Ⓐ She thought her parents would not listen.
- Ⓑ She was too ashamed.
- Ⓒ The bully told Tia not to tell.
- Ⓓ Tia did not know about the bully.

_____ ❺ **What caused the bully to leave Tia alone?**
- Ⓐ Tia grew.
- Ⓑ Tia asked the bully to stop what she was doing.
- Ⓒ Tia moved.
- Ⓓ Tia's parents made the bully stop.

_____ ❻ **The new girl was probably afraid of Tia because _____**
- Ⓐ Tia got in a lot of trouble.
- Ⓑ Tia bullied her.
- Ⓒ Tia was picked on by a bully.
- Ⓓ Tia was bigger than her.

Word Power

Choose the English word from the Vocabulary list that correctly matches the definition.

embarrassed

_____

a person who teases, hurts, or threatens others

_____

to pardon, or accept, a wrong action done by someone else

_____

to laugh at someone or say unkind things about him or her

_____

LESSON 13
Captions to Determine Main Ideas

Reading Tip

 Please follow the instructions in Part 1 and Part 2 before you listen to and read the passage.

 There are two captions in this lesson. If you read only the captions, would you know what the passage is about? How do the captions explain what the passage is about?

HINE, LEWIS WICKES/ LIBRARY OF CONGRESS

Long ago, everyone in the family worked.

Families Then and Now

Skill Overview

A caption is one or more sentences that summarize a photograph or an illustration. Sometimes, a caption is one or two words used as a title for the picture. The picture caption extends the reader's knowledge of the picture. It also gives important information that adds to the main idea of the text.

Today, families also work but have more free time to spend with each other.

🎧 13

Long ago, people lived and worked in cities, towns, and the country. Children studied, did **chores**, and played when they could. Families ate meals together and went to church together. They took care of each other.

Families then and now are not so different from each other. They are the same in the most important ways, like **caring for** and loving each other. But they are different in some ways, too.

Long ago, adults worked hard all day long. Many men were farmers. They cared for **crops** and animals, made **repairs**, and **provided** food for their families. Women cared for the homes and children. They prepared food. They cleaned, sewed, and **spun thread**.

Adults today work hard, too. But they usually don't work for so long. They have a lot more time off. Stores and **inventions** make life easier, as well. For example, most people buy food and clothes at stores. Some adults work away from home and spend the rest of the time with their families. Others work at home and take care of their families at the same time.

Vocabulary

chore
specific piece of work that one is required to do as a duty

⭐ **care for someone**
to protect someone or something and provide the things the person needs

crop
a cultivated plant that is grown on a large scale commercially

repair
to fix something

provide
to give

spin
to turn or whirl around quickly

thread
a long, thin strand of cotton, nylon, or other fiber used in sewing or weaving

invention
something new that has been created to make daily life easier or better

Reading Skill Comprehension Practice

Part 1

Read the caption under the picture on the first page of this lesson. "Long ago, everyone in the family worked." Explain what this tells you about the **main idea** of the passage.

_____

_____

Part 2

Read the caption under the picture on the second page of this lesson. "Today, families also work but have more free time to spend with each other." Explain what this tells you about the **main idea** of the passage.

_____

_____

Part 3 Write a new caption for each of the main pictures in the passage.

_____   _____

_____   _____

Comprehension Review

Fill in the best answer for each question.

❶ The caption at the top of the second page tells you that today's families _____

Ⓐ have no free time.
Ⓑ have more free time.
Ⓒ do not work.
Ⓓ are just like families long ago.

❷ Which describes families long ago?
Ⓐ Only the parents worked.
Ⓑ People had free time.
Ⓒ Everyone in the family worked.
Ⓓ Most people did not work.

❸ The captions tell you that this passage is *mostly* about _____
Ⓐ families then and now.
Ⓑ how people build houses.
Ⓒ life in the city.
Ⓓ how families grew crops long ago.

❹ Like families long ago, today's families _____
Ⓐ have free time.
Ⓑ care for and love each other.
Ⓒ work hard all day long.
Ⓓ buy clothes and food at stores.

❺ Unlike today's families, families long ago _____
Ⓐ did not care for and love each other.
Ⓑ bought their clothes and food at stores.
Ⓒ did not farm.
Ⓓ did not have stores and inventions to make life easier.

❻ Which statement is true about today's adults?
Ⓐ They do not take care of their families.
Ⓑ They have no free time.
Ⓒ They have more time off than adults who lived long ago.
Ⓓ They do not work hard.

Word Power

Choose the English word from the Vocabulary list that correctly matches the definition.

 specific piece of work that one is required to do as a duty

_____

 to give

_____

 something new that has been created to make daily life easier or better

_____

 to fix something

_____

55

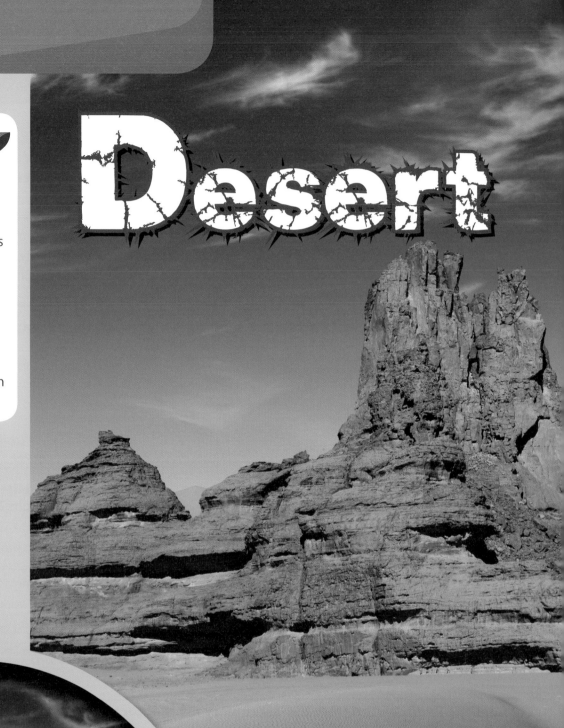

Desert

Reading Tip

- Please pay special attention to the diagram. Looking at the diagram as well as reading the passage will enhance your understanding of evaporation.

- Think about how the diagram helps you to comprehend the main idea of the passage.

Skill Overview

Graphic features include graphs, tables, charts, diagrams, sketches, flowcharts, photographs, and time lines. **Graphic features** can help tell the main idea of the passage and enhance reading comprehension.

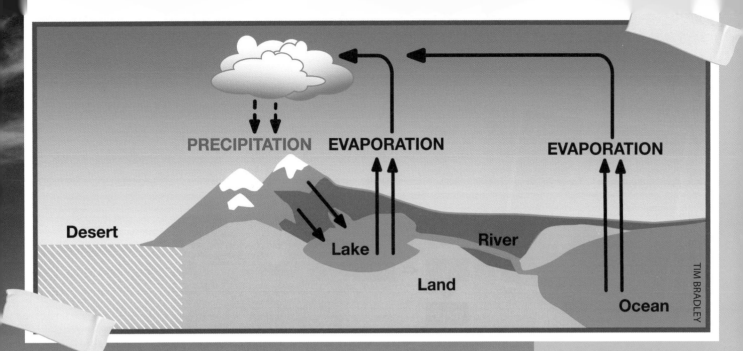

PRECIPITATION   EVAPORATION   EVAPORATION

Desert

Lake

River

Land

Ocean

TIM BRADLEY

What Is a Desert?

A desert is an area of land with very little rain and, most of the time, high temperatures during the day.

In a desert, there is less than 10 inches (25.4 cm) of rain each year. The ground is usually **dry**. Whenever it does rain in a desert, the heat of the sun dries up most of the water again. This is called **evaporation**.

One reason for evaporation is the **extreme temperatures**. Desert nights can be very cold. This is because the ground **releases** its heat at night. During the day, the ground soaks up the heat. The temperature in the desert can reach 130°F (54°C). How hot is that? Most people are comfortable at about 70°F (21°C). Deserts can get almost twice that hot!

How Is a Desert Formed?

Many deserts are **formed** because of mountains. High mountains keep **moisture** from getting past them. Rain and snow fall on the mountains, but the air is dry by the time it gets to the desert.

Some deserts are formed because the land is far away from bodies of water. The air soaks up water from lakes and oceans, but then it rains long before it gets to the desert. The rain cannot make it that far.

power up There are different kinds of graphic features.

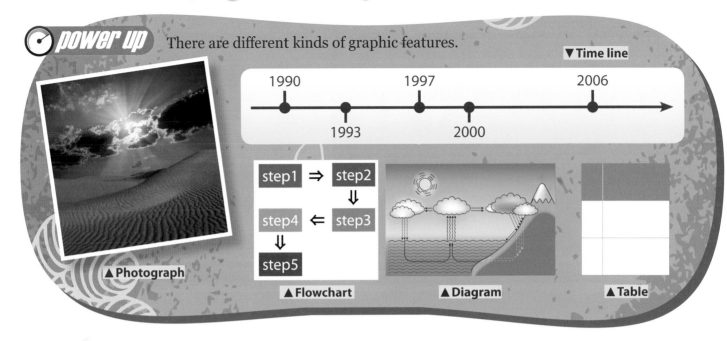

▲ Photograph   ▲ Flowchart   ▲ Diagram   ▲ Table

▼ Time line
1990   1997   2006
1993   2000

step1 ⇒ step2
⇓
step4 ⇐ step3
⇓
step5

Part 1 Write something you learned from the diagram.

I learned that one of the reasons water evaporates in the desert is the extreme temperatures.

Part 2 Look at the diagram on page 57 and answer the following questions.

1
What does the diagram show?

2
What happens to water in lakes and oceans?

3
How does water get from a lake to the ocean?

4
What is precipitation?

Part 3 The main idea is the overall message or important idea that the author wants to convey. Please state the main idea of the diagram.

Comprehension Review

Fill in the best answer for each question.

_____ ❶ The diagram tells you that some water evaporates from _____
- Ⓐ lakes.
- Ⓑ mountains.
- Ⓒ land.
- Ⓓ clouds.

_____ ❷ The diagram shows that rain falls _mostly_ _____
- Ⓐ by rivers.
- Ⓑ near the ocean.
- Ⓒ on land.
- Ⓓ near mountains.

_____ ❸ What is another word for _rain_?
- Ⓐ evaporation
- Ⓑ precipitation
- Ⓒ ocean
- Ⓓ temperature

_____ ❹ Which does _not_ cause deserts to form?
- Ⓐ high mountains
- Ⓑ land that is far away from water
- Ⓒ heavy rains
- Ⓓ rain falling before it can get to the desert

_____ ❺ What is it called when the sun dries up water?
- Ⓐ evaporation
- Ⓑ a body of water
- Ⓒ precipitation
- Ⓓ rain

_____ ❻ What causes desert nights to be cold?
- Ⓐ The ground soaks up rain.
- Ⓑ The ground is usually dry.
- Ⓒ High mountains keep moisture from getting past them.
- Ⓓ The ground releases its heat at night.

Word Power

Choose the English word from the Vocabulary list that correctly matches the definition.

1. the process by which water dries up

_____

2. to create

_____

3. water or the amount of water that falls to Earth as hail, mist, rain, sleet, or snow

4. reaching a high or highest degree; very great

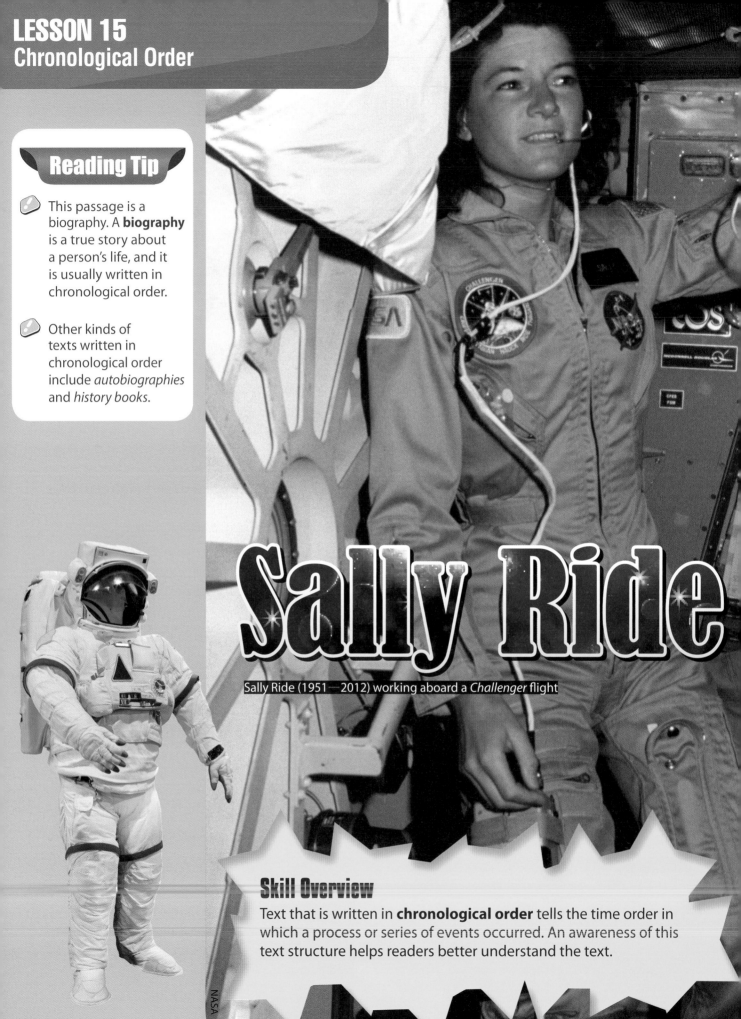

Reading Tip

This passage is a biography. A **biography** is a true story about a person's life, and it is usually written in chronological order.

Other kinds of texts written in chronological order include *autobiographies* and *history books*.

Sally Ride

Sally Ride (1951—2012) working aboard a *Challenger* flight

Skill Overview

Text that is written in **chronological order** tells the time order in which a process or series of events occurred. An awareness of this text structure helps readers better understand the text.

NASA

It takes special people to be **astronauts**. These people must be healthy and strong. They must be good learners. They must be good at math and science. They must be good problem solvers. These people must want to succeed. And they also need to work well with others to meet goals. One of these special people is Sally Ride.

Sally Ride was born on May 26, 1951, in Los Angeles, California. As a child, she tried many things. She played football and baseball with the boys. She was often the only girl allowed to play. Sally's mother asked her to try tennis. Sally went on to become a highly ranked tennis player. In high school, she met a teacher who **encouraged** her to become a scientist.

In college, Sally had two loves: tennis and science. She could have become a pro tennis player, but she chose science instead. She went on to study at Stanford University. There, she read an ad by NASA (National Aeronautics and Space Administration). They were looking for young scientists to become astronauts.

This ad was a **turning point** in her life. More than 8,000 people applied to NASA. Sally was one of only 35 people chosen that year. Sally worked and studied hard while training as an astronaut. The people at NASA **respected** her. Then in 1982, all her hard work paid off. She was picked to be on the **crew** of the seventh space shuttle flight. Sally Ride would be the first American woman in space!

On the Challenger flight, she **operated** a robotlike arm. This arm helped the crew work with satellites. She **proved** herself to be the best person for the job—man or woman. Sally also flew with the 1984 Challenger crew. But in 1986, tragedy struck. The tenth shuttle mission of the Challenger exploded after takeoff. All seven crew members were killed. Sally was part of a team that studied the accident. Soon after, she left the astronaut program to work at Stanford University.

Sally Ride aimed at being the best she could be and became it. She is an example to young people around the world to seek what they dream. Sally Ride has earned her place in the history of space **exploration**.

Vocabulary

astronaut
a person who has been trained for traveling in space

encourage
to try to persuade a person to do something

☆**turning point**
a time at which a decisive change in a situation occurs

respect
to think very highly of

crew
a group of people who work together on a project

operate
to work, be in action, or have an effect

prove
to show a particular result after a period of time

exploration
the activity of searching and finding out about something

Reading Skill Comprehension Practice

Part 1

List three types of text that are typically written in chronological order.

- ✓ _autobiographies_
- ✓ _____
- ✓ _____
- ✓ _____

Part 2

Please refer to the passage and identify some important events in Sally Ride's life. Match an important event that occurred in her life to each date shown on the time line.

Sally Ride, First American Woman in Space

1984 _____

1982 _____

1951 _____

Part 3

Think of two other events that you would like to add to the time line in Part 2. List them below.

1. _The year Sally Ride was accepted by NASA._

2. _____

3. _____

Comprehension Review

Fill in the best answer for each question.

_____ **❶ Which one happened *last*?**
- Ⓐ Sally Ride flew with the 1984 Challenger crew.
- Ⓑ Sally Ride became a highly ranked tennis player.
- Ⓒ Sally Ride studied at Stanford.
- Ⓓ Sally Ride trained to be an astronaut.

_____ **❷ Sally Ride studied science at Stanford University *after* _____**
- Ⓐ she flew with the 1984 Challenger crew.
- Ⓑ she read an ad by NASA.
- Ⓒ she became a highly ranked tennis player.
- Ⓓ she trained to be an astronaut.

_____ **❸ Sally Ride flew with the 1984 Challenger crew *before* _____**
- Ⓐ she studied at Stanford University.
- Ⓑ she earned her place in the history of space exploration.
- Ⓒ she got accepted by NASA.
- Ⓓ she was encouraged to become a scientist.

_____ **❹ People who like _____ would probably read this passage.**
- Ⓐ science
- Ⓑ math
- Ⓒ dinosaurs
- Ⓓ novels

_____ **❺ This passage is a _____**
- Ⓐ fictional story.
- Ⓑ diary entry.
- Ⓒ biography.
- Ⓓ science experiment.

_____ **❻ Which word best describes Sally Ride?**
- Ⓐ arrogant
- Ⓑ lazy
- Ⓒ peaceful
- Ⓓ ambitious

Word Power

Choose the English word from the Vocabulary list that correctly matches the definition.

1   a group of people who work together on a project

_____

2   to try to persuade a person to do something

_____

3   to think very highly of

_____

4   the activity of searching and finding out about something

_____

ART OF AFRICA

Skill Overview

The elements of story structure are the characters, plot, and setting. The structure provides readers with an understanding of how stories are created and can help them make accurate predictions when reading new stories.

🎧 16

African art has a long history. The oldest works of art date back to 6000 B.C. These include rock paintings and engravings. African art shows the cultural **diversity** of Africa's people. There are many traditional types of African art. They include **textiles** and jewelry.

African Fiber Art

Africans love color, patterns, and **texture**. This can be seen in every part of their lives. In the rain forest, bark is taken from trees. The bark is then soaked and beaten. It is used to form **fabric**. This fabric is used for clothes. The Mbuti (em-BOO-tee) women get dyes from plants. They use the dyes to paint each sheet. Elsewhere, **fibers** are stripped and dyed. Then it is **woven** into cloth. The ancient Egyptians used the fibers of the flax plant. They wove the fibers into fine white cloth called *linen*.

Kente is a beautiful fabric from Ghana. First, it was made from raffia (dried grass). Later, it was made from silk. Kente cloth is made on a loom in long strips. The strips are then woven together. The patterns are complex. Each pattern has a name that tells about its meaning.

African Jewelry

Jewelry plays an important role in Africa. Women, men, and children wear jewelry. The jewelry can have many designs. It is worn on many parts of the body. It has special meanings in each **tribe**. Some jewelry is worn only on special days, such as weddings. Other pieces are given as gifts, such as friendship bracelets. Each piece shows the wealth and status of the owner.

There are many traditional **materials** used for jewelry. These include fur, shells, ivory, glass, and more. Metals may also be used for jewelry. Some metals used are gold, tin, copper, and silver.

You may wish to find out about other forms of African art like sculpture, furniture, and pottery.

◀ Masai woman's jewelry

Vocabulary

diversity
a mixture of many different types

textile
a cloth made by hand or machine

texture
how something feels when touched

fabric
cloth or material for making clothes, covering furniture, etc.

fiber
any of the threadlike parts that form plant or artificial material and can be made into cloth

weave
to put together into a pattern by going over and under (as with thread or yarn)

tribe
a group of people who live together, sharing the same language, culture, and history, especially those who do not live in towns or cities

material
solid substance such as fabric, wood, or metal

Reading Skill Comprehension Practice

 **Part 1**

Look at the title, headings, and pictures that go with this passage. Predict what you will read about in this lesson. Then listen to and read the first paragraph.

The Art of Africa
African Fiber Art
African Jewelry

Based on the title, headings, and pictures, I think the passage will describe the art of Africa.

 **Part 2** After reading the first paragraph, add more details to your prediction to show what you have learned.

The passage will talk about African art, especially its textiles and jewelry.

 **Part 3** Make a prediction about the section of text with the heading **African Fiber Art**.

This section will talk about what African fabric art is famous for.

 **Part 4** Make a prediction about the section of text with the heading **African Jewelry**.

This section will provide different kinds of African jewelry as examples.

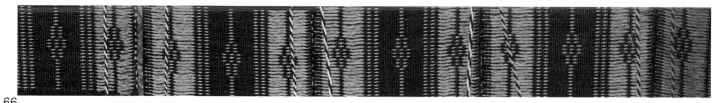

Comprehension Review

Fill in the best answer for each question.

_____ ❶ **"African Jewelry"**
This heading tells that you will read about _____

Ⓐ the history of Africa.

Ⓑ why African jewelry is important in Africa.

Ⓒ how plants are used to make cloth.

Ⓓ how to make beaded jewelry.

_____ ❷ **"Africans love color, patterns, and texture."**
This topic sentence tells you that this paragraph is _mostly_ about _____

Ⓐ African fiber art.   Ⓒ jewelry.

Ⓑ linen.   Ⓓ the people of Ghana.

_____ ❸ **In this passage, you will _not_ read about _____**

Ⓐ the special meanings of African art.

Ⓑ the colors, patterns, and textures of fiber art.

Ⓒ materials used to make African jewelry.

Ⓓ traditional African dances.

_____ ❹ **Which statement is _not_ true of African jewelry?**

Ⓐ It is often given as a gift.

Ⓑ It is worn on many parts of the body.

Ⓒ It usually has one simple design.

Ⓓ It shows the wealth and status of the owner.

_____ ❺ **The purpose of this passage is _____**

Ⓐ to get you to wear more jewelry.

Ⓑ to share about the art of Africa.

Ⓒ to get you to visit Africa.

Ⓓ to tell the history of Africa.

_____ ❻ **The graphic features in this passage show you that African art is _____**

Ⓐ colorful.

Ⓑ dark.

Ⓒ simple.

Ⓓ expensive.

Word Power

Choose the English word from the Vocabulary list that correctly matches the definition.

 solid substance such as fabric, wood, or metal

_____

 to put together into a pattern by going over and under (as with thread or yarn)

_____

 how something feels when touched

_____

 cloth or material for making clothes, covering furniture, etc.

_____

THE GRANGER COLLECTION, NEW YORK

▲ Eleanor Roosevelt

Reading Tip

An author's purpose is the reason why he or she writes a text. Think about what the author's purpose was for writing this passage.

Champion for Change

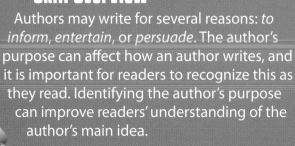

Skill Overview

Authors may write for several reasons: *to inform, entertain,* or *persuade.* The author's purpose can affect how an author writes, and it is important for readers to recognize this as they read. Identifying the author's purpose can improve readers' understanding of the author's main idea.

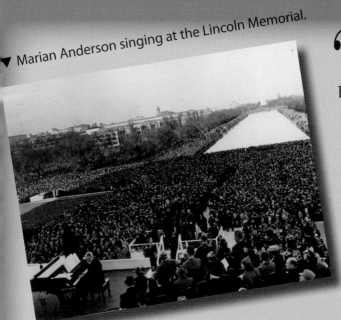

▼ Marian Anderson singing at the Lincoln Memorial.

🎧 17

The year 1920 brought a huge **victory** for women. This was the year the suffrage battle was won—women could now **vote**. There was one woman who broke all the rules. She fought for **equal rights** for everyone. She set her own **goals** as the wife of a president. Her name was Eleanor Roosevelt.

Eleanor Roosevelt

In the 1930s, many people treated African Americans unfairly. Eleanor saw that African Americans could not go to the same schools as whites. They could not eat at the same places. Some towns even kept them from voting.

As First Lady, she knew she had to do something about this. Eleanor asked politicians to work for **civil rights**. She never gave up. She wanted all people to have the same rights.

Helping Marian Anderson

▼ Marian Anderson

Marian Anderson was a well-known singer during the 1930s. She had a great voice. She was a big **success**. Anderson planned to sing at a popular place in Washington, D.C. She was told she could not sing there because she was African American. Eleanor Roosevelt was angry about this, so she found a way for Anderson to sing somewhere else in Washington, D.C. This special place was the Lincoln Memorial. She sang in front of more than 75,000 people. She ended with the song "America." One line in that song says, "From every mountainside, let **freedom** ring." It was a special moment for everyone there.

Reading Skill Comprehension Practice

 An author's purpose may be to inform, to entertain, or to persuade.

To inform
means to provide readers with <u>information or knowledge</u>.

To entertain
means to provide readers with <u>amusement or enjoyment</u>.

To persuade
means to <u>convince readers</u> or to <u>make them believe in something</u>.

Part 1

After reading the passage, please write at least three things you have learned from it. This can be something related to Eleanor Roosevelt, something about Marian Anderson, and so on.

1. *As the wife of the president, Eleanor Roosevelt fought for equal rights for everyone.*

2. _____

3. _____

4. _____

Part 2

Do you think the author was trying to entertain you by writing this passage? Explain your answer.

_____

_____

_____

Part 3   Answer the questions below.

(YES) (NO) **1.** Do you think the author wrote the passage to persuade you to feel a certain way?

2. If so, what was the author trying to persuade you to think?

_____

(YES) (NO) **3.** Was the author successful?

Comprehension Review

Fill in the best answer for each question.

_____ **❶ The author wrote this passage to _____**

Ⓐ teach you the words to "America."

Ⓑ get you to visit the Lincoln Memorial.

Ⓒ describe Eleanor Roosevelt's fight for civil rights.

Ⓓ share a personal story.

_____ **❷ The author wants you to _____**

Ⓐ know about Eleanor Roosevelt.

Ⓑ buy Marian Anderson's music.

Ⓒ visit Washington, D.C.

Ⓓ learn the history of the Lincoln Memorial.

_____ **❸ The author wanted to _____**

Ⓐ share a poem.

Ⓑ tell about a person.

Ⓒ give a list of instructions.

Ⓓ share a diary entry.

_____ **❹ Which is an opinion?**

Ⓐ Marian Anderson was a well-known singer during the 1930s.

Ⓑ She sang in front of more than 75,000 people.

Ⓒ She ended with the song "America."

Ⓓ She had a great voice.

_____ **❺ Which of these did Eleanor Roosevelt do to fight for civil rights?**

Ⓐ She sang at a popular place in Washington, D.C.

Ⓑ She sang at the Lincoln Memorial.

Ⓒ She asked politicians to work for civil rights.

Ⓓ She made new civil rights laws.

_____ **❻ Which is the main idea in this passage?**

Ⓐ Eleanor Roosevelt wanted Marian Anderson to sing.

Ⓑ Eleanor Roosevelt wanted equal rights for everyone.

Ⓒ Marian Anderson was a very popular singer.

Ⓓ Eleanor Roosevelt was the First Lady.

Word Power

Choose the English word from the Vocabulary list that correctly matches the definition.

the fair claim to be allowed to do certain things

_____

being the same in quantity, size, degree, or value

_____

the thing that people try to achieve or accomplish

_____

people's rights

_____

Reading Tip

Please follow the instructions in Part 1 before you listen to and read the passage.

"Focus on Hispanic Americans" is the book title of this passage. The book is about people of Hispanic origin who have lived in America.

"Chapter 3: Roberto Clemente, A Great Man" is the chapter title of this passage.

MLB PHOTOS / GETTY IMAGES

Focus on Hispanic Americans

Skill Overview
Chapter titles outline the text and help guide readers to the categories that frame a book. The title of a chapter gives information about the main idea of the chapter.

Roberto Clemente, A Great Man

Roberto Clemente loved baseball. He grew up in Carolina, Puerto Rico. There, he played every chance he could get. While listening to the radio, he would squeeze a ball to build up the muscles in his throwing arm. He would bounce a rubber ball off the wall to practice catching. Sometimes, he and his friends could not buy real baseballs. So, they made their own. They used old golf balls, string, and tape.

As Roberto grew older, he practiced more. Because of this, he became a better baseball player. Roberto was **offered** a job with the Brooklyn Dodgers, but his father said he had to finish school. After finishing school, he went to Montreal, Canada. He played on a farm team there. Some **pro** teams came to watch him play. The Pittsburgh Pirates soon asked him to play right field for their team. Roberto accepted.

As a Pirate, Roberto was on two teams that won the World Series. He was the Most **Valuable** Player in the 1971 World Series. He had more than 3,000 hits in his **career**. As a **champion**, Roberto never forgot his fans. He thanked his fans instead of going to parties with his teammates. He **donated** money to needy people. He spent time visiting sick children. When an earthquake struck Nicaragua, he spent the Christmas holiday collecting **supplies** for the victims. He was going to fly from Puerto Rico to Nicaragua on December 31, 1972, to **deliver** the supplies. Shortly after the plane took off, it crashed. Roberto and everybody else on the plane died.

Roberto was missed by many people. Three months after he died, he was voted into the Baseball Hall of Fame. Roberto's father wanted him to be a good man. Roberto proved to be a great man.

Vocabulary

offer
to ask someone if they would like to have something

pro
abbreviation of *professional*

valuable
worth a lot of money

career
an occupation undertaken for a significant period of a person's life

champion
a person who achieves something great

donate
to give something valuable without asking for anything in return

supplies
materials that are needed or wanted

deliver
to take goods, letters, parcels, etc., to people's houses or places of work

Reading Skill Comprehension Practice

The main idea of a passage is what the passage is about. Read the book title and the chapter title of this passage. Predict the main idea of the passage based on these titles.

Book Title	Chapter Title
Focus on Hispanic Americans	Chapter 3: Roberto Clemente, A Great Man

Reread the passage and identify the behaviors and actions that made Clemente a great man. List at least three of the actions and behaviors that people considered special.

1. _He was picked up by the Pittsburgh Pirates to play right field for the team._

2. _____

3. _____

4. _____

 Now that you have read the passage, determine the main idea. Write your own version of the main idea for the passage below.

_____
_____
_____

Comprehension Review

Fill in the best answer for each question.

_____ **❶ The chapter title tells that you will read about _____**

Ⓐ baseball.

Ⓑ Latin America.

Ⓒ Roberto Clemente.

Ⓓ the Pittsburgh Pirates.

_____ **❷ Information about _____ will probably *not* be in this passage.**

Ⓐ Roberto Clemente's life

Ⓑ basketball stars

Ⓒ Roberto Clemente's career

Ⓓ baseball

_____ **❸ The chapter title tells you that this passage is *mostly* about _____**

Ⓐ Roberto Clemente's achievements.

Ⓑ Roberto Clemente's baseball statistics.

Ⓒ Roberto Clemente's hometown.

Ⓓ the Baseball Hall of Fame.

_____ **❹ Which word *best* describes Roberto Clemente?**

Ⓐ selfish

Ⓑ funny

Ⓒ fearless

Ⓓ generous

_____ **❺ Roberto Clemente played baseball for the _____**

Ⓐ Boston Red Sox.

Ⓑ Brooklyn Dodgers.

Ⓒ Pittsburgh Pirates.

Ⓓ New York Yankees.

_____ **❻ Roberto Clemente played on a farm team in Canada *after* _____**

Ⓐ he got the MVP award in the 1971 World Series.

Ⓑ he was offered a job with the Brooklyn Dodgers.

Ⓒ he agreed to play for the Pittsburgh Pirates.

Ⓓ he flew to Nicaragua in 1972.

Word Power

Choose the English word from the Vocabulary list that correctly matches the definition.

a person who achieves something great

_____

to give something valuable without asking for anything in return

_____

materials that are needed or wanted

_____

to take goods, letters, parcels, etc., to people's houses or places of work

_____

LESSON 19
Logical Order

Reading Tip

Different kinds of texts require different kinds of organizational structure. This passage tells the reader how to build something, so it must be written in step-by-step order.

Skill Overview

Authors structure, or organize, the information in their writing so that it makes sense to the reader. Text that is written in a logical order explains information in a way that makes sense, based on the given topic.

Building a Birdhouse

 Make Sure Your *Kit* Has These Parts:

2 roof pieces

1 end piece, with pointed top and two holes

1 end piece, with pointed top

1 round **perch**

2 side pieces

1 floor piece

1 metal chain

1 tube of wood glue

2 wood *screws*

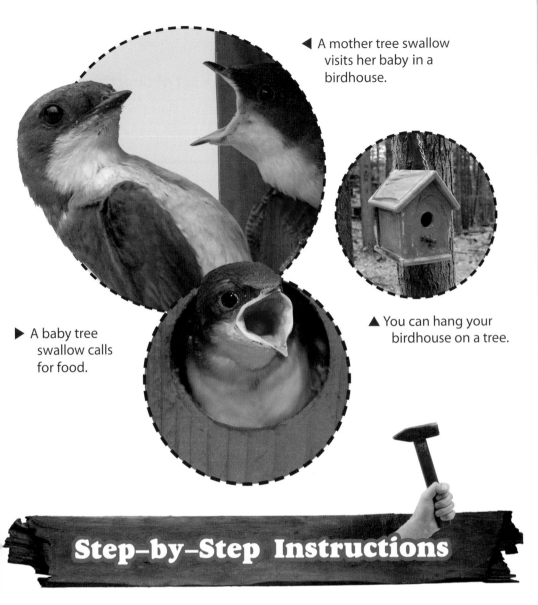

◀ A mother tree swallow visits her baby in a birdhouse.

▶ A baby tree swallow calls for food.

▲ You can hang your birdhouse on a tree.

▲ a nest

Step-by-Step Instructions

1. Place the floor piece flat. Glue the two side pieces to it at a 90-degree **angle**.

2. Glue the front and end pieces to the three pieces.

3. Glue the two roof pieces in place. Let it sit overnight or until the glue is dry.

4. Push the round perch into the small hole on the front of the birdhouse.

5. **Fasten** the metal chain to the roof by putting the wood screws in the two predrilled holes.

6. Now, find a **secluded** spot under a tree or under the **eaves** of your roof. Hang your birdhouse. Soon, you will have a family of happy birds **nesting** there.

7. Use a pair of binoculars to watch the happy family of birds that will be nesting there.

77

Reading Skill Comprehension Practice

 **Part 1** Write about your experience reading and following a set of directions, such as a manual or a recipe.

I followed a set of directions when I was installing my new mirror last weekend. I looked at the parts needed and the equipment required. I followed the directions exactly, so I successfully set up the new mirror in my bedroom.

_____

_____

_____

_____

 **Part 2** Reread the passage to answer questions about assembling a birdhouse. Please answer in complete sentences.

1. How many tubes of wood glue do you need?

_____

2. What does step 4 tell you to do?

_____

3. Where should you hang your birdhouse?

_____

4. How many side pieces do you need for this project?

_____

 **Part 3** Match the type of text on the right with the text structure on the left. Some structures may be used more than once.

Text Structure	Type of Text
A. similar items are grouped together	_____ **1.** a phone book
B. alphabetical order	_____ **2.** a biography of George Washington
C. compare and contrast	_____ **3.** a menu
D. sequential order	_____ **4.** a bus schedule
	_____ **5.** a book about frogs and toads

Comprehension Review

Fill in the best answer for each question.

_____ **❶ Glue the side pieces to the floor piece *before* you _____**
- Ⓐ make sure your kit has all the parts.
- Ⓑ place the floor piece flat.
- Ⓒ glue the front and end pieces to the three other pieces.
- Ⓓ read the instructions.

_____ **❷ *After* you fasten the metal chain to the roof, _____**
- Ⓐ place the floor piece flat.
- Ⓑ hang your birdhouse.
- Ⓒ glue the front and end pieces to the three pieces.
- Ⓓ let it sit until the glue dries.

_____ **❸ The *first* step in making a birdhouse is to_____**
- Ⓐ push the round perch into the small hole on the front of the birdhouse.
- Ⓑ glue the front and end pieces to the three pieces.
- Ⓒ hang your birdhouse.
- Ⓓ place the floor piece flat.

_____ **❹ Which is not a part of the birdhouse kit?**
- Ⓐ 1 tube of wood glue
- Ⓑ a pair of binoculars
- Ⓒ 2 side pieces
- Ⓓ 1 round perch

_____ **❺ "*Now, find a secluded spot under a tree or under the eaves of your roof.*"**
What is another word for *secluded*?
- Ⓐ hidden
- Ⓒ loud
- Ⓑ icy
- Ⓓ busy

_____ **❻ You would read this passage if you wanted to _____**
- Ⓐ buy a new house.
- Ⓑ read about different trees.
- Ⓒ learn about birds.
- Ⓓ learn how to make a birdhouse.

Word Power

Choose the English word from the Vocabulary list that correctly matches the definition.

 1 the lower edge of a roof that sticks out beyond the wall of a house or building
_____

 2 a place for a bird to sit
_____

 3 secret or hidden from view
_____

 4 a set of things, such as tools or clothes, used for a particular purpose or activity
_____

79

The Sugar Maple Tree

Skill Overview

Facts are true statements, while **opinions** reflect one's feelings or emotions. Readers must be able to distinguish between fact and opinion in order to read a text critically and understand the author's point of view.

The sugar maple is a great tree. Maple **syrup** and maple sugar are made from its **sap**. The wood of the maple makes pretty furniture and cabinets. It also makes a fine **shade** tree. People plant sugar maples around their houses. They also plant them along their streets.

The leaves of the sugar maple turn a **rich** yellow, orange, or deep red in the fall. They look like someone painted them with a giant brush. In the winter, the tree loses its leaves. Then it is **bare**.

The **bark** of the tree is **flaky** and gray. Its **seeds** are eaten by birds, squirrels, and other small animals.

The sugar maple grows 75—100 feet (22.9—30.4 m) tall. There are many kinds of maple trees. The black maple, red maple, and silver maple are just a few of the 60 kinds. But if you are looking for an excellent tree to plant in your yard, choose the sugar maple.

▼ The bark of the maple tree is flaky and gray.

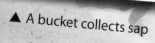
▲ A bucket collects sap

Vocabulary

syrup
a very sweet, thick, light-colored liquid

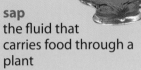

sap
the fluid that carries food through a plant

shade
slight darkness caused by something blocking direct light from the sun

rich
deep in color

bare
uncovered

bark
the hard outer covering of a tree

flaky
coming off easily in small, flat, thin pieces

seed
the unit of reproduction of a flowering plant

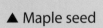
▲ Maple seed

 **Part 1** Read the following statements. Check the passage to see whether they are true or false. Write a "T" next to the sentence if it is true. Write an "F" next to the sentence if it is false.

1

2

3

_____ The bark of the sugar maple tree is dark brown.

_____ There are 20 varieties of sugar maple trees.

_____ Maple syrup is made from sap.

 **Part 2** Review the passage. Write four words from the passage that show a statement is an opinion.

> impressive

>

>

Opinion Words

> fabulous

>

>

 **Part 3** Write three facts and three opinions from the passage.

▶ Facts ◀	▶ Opinions ◀
1. Maple syrup is made from the sap of the sugar maple.	1. The sugar maple is a great tree.
2.	2.
3.	3.
4.	4.

Comprehension Review

Fill in the best answer for each question.

_____ **1** **Which statement is a fact?**
ⓐ In the winter, the tree loses its leaves.
ⓑ The sugar maple is a great tree.
ⓒ The wood of the maple makes pretty furniture and cabinets.
ⓓ It also makes a fine shade tree.

_____ **2** **Which statement is an opinion?**
ⓐ People plant sugar maples around their houses.
ⓑ There are many kinds of maple trees.
ⓒ The wood of the maple makes pretty furniture and cabinets.
ⓓ The bark of the tree is flaky and gray.

_____ **3** **The author thinks that** _____
ⓐ maple syrup and maple sugar are made from its sap.
ⓑ the black maple, red maple, and silver maple are just a few of the 60 kinds.
ⓒ the sugar maple grows mainly in the middle and eastern states.
ⓓ the sugar maple is a great tree.

_____ **4** **This passage is** _____
ⓐ a letter.
ⓑ an informational text.
ⓒ a personal story.
ⓓ an editorial.

_____ **5** **Which is _not_ a use for sugar maples?**
ⓐ cars
ⓑ shade
ⓒ furniture
ⓓ syrup

_____ **6** **The author** _____
ⓐ thinks sugar maples are ugly trees.
ⓑ would never want a sugar maple.
ⓒ has never seen a sugar maple.
ⓓ probably has a sugar maple.

Word Power

Choose the English word from the Vocabulary list that correctly matches the definition.

1 the fluid that carries food through a plant

_____

2 deep in color

_____

3 uncovered

_____

4 a very sweet, thick, light-colored liquid

_____

The Ant and the Chrysalis

Skill Overview

Self-monitoring allows readers to make sure they understand a text. Readers who monitor themselves understand when they are confused by a section of text, when a text does not make sense, and when they are reading too fast or too slowly.

An ant running about in the sunshine in search of food came across a **chrysalis**. It was very near its time of **metamorphosis**. The chrysalis moved its tail and **attracted** the ant's attention. The ant saw for the first time that it was alive. "Poor, pitiful animal! What a sad fate is yours! I can run here and there, as I please. And, if I wish, I can climb the tallest tree. You lie **imprisoned** here in your **shell**. And you only have the power to move a joint or two of your scaly tail," the ant said. The chrysalis heard all this, but did not try to make any reply.

A few days later, the ant passed that way again. But this time, nothing but the shell remained. The ant wondered what had happened to its contents. Suddenly, he felt himself shaded and fanned by the **gorgeous** wings of a beautiful butterfly.

"Look at me, your much-pitied friend! **Boast** now of your powers to run and climb! But it will be difficult for me to listen," said the **monarch**. After he said this, the butterfly rose high in the air. Soon, he was lost to the sight of the ant forever.

The moral of this fable is: Appearances are deceiving.

21

Vocabulary

- **chrysalis**
  an insect covered by a hard case at the stage of development before it becomes a moth or butterfly with wings

- **metamorphosis**
  a process of changing from one form to another (as in a chrysalis into a butterfly)

  attract
  to pull or draw someone or something toward yourself or toward itself

  imprisoned
  closed in, with no escape

  shell
  a hard, protective outer case

  gorgeous
  very beautiful or pleasant

  boast
  to brag

  monarch
  a kind of butterfly

Reading Skill Comprehension Practice

Tell what you were thinking as you listened to and read the passage. What kind of questions did you have? Were you confused by parts of the story?

I was thinking that it would be very interesting if an ant could talk to a butterfly in reality.

_____

_____

The checklist offers self-monitoring tips and questions that you might want to think about as you read a text. Reread the passage and fill in this checklist to help you monitor your reading.

YES	NO	Questions
		1. Did all the words make sense?
		2. Did you understand the events in the story?
		3. Were you able to stay focused while reading?
		4. Did the story make you think about something you already knew?
		5. Did the passage remind you of another story?
		6. Did you have a picture in your head while you read?

Reread the passage. Please mark the text when you encounter a new word or phrase. Write down the words or phrases which are confusing to you.

1.	4.
2.	5.
3.	6.

Comprehension Review

Fill in the best answer for each question.

_____ ❶ **"The chrysalis moved its tail and attracted the ant's attention."**
If you did not know what _attracted_ means, what could you do?
Ⓐ Read the title.
Ⓑ Spell the word out loud.
Ⓒ Write the word.
Ⓓ Look up the word in a dictionary.

_____ ❷ **"The ant wondered what had happened to its contents."**
What is a good way to find out what had happened to the chrysalis?
Ⓐ Read the sentence again. Ⓒ Read the rest of the story.
Ⓑ Read the title. Ⓓ Look up the word _contents_.

_____ ❸ **What can help you understand what the chrysalis and butterfly looked like?**
Ⓐ reading the title
Ⓑ looking at the pictures
Ⓒ reading key words
Ⓓ spelling the words _chrysalis_ and _butterfly_

_____ ❹ **What is another way to say "appearances are deceiving"?**
Ⓐ Things are not always what they seem to be.
Ⓑ Do not trust a butterfly.
Ⓒ Ants cannot see.
Ⓓ Be careful of ants.

_____ ❺ **Where did the butterfly come from?**
Ⓐ a leaf from a tree
Ⓑ the ant
Ⓒ the chrysalis
Ⓓ a cloud

_____ ❻ **At first, the ant feels _____ the chrysalis.**
Ⓐ afraid of
Ⓑ sorry for
Ⓒ proud of
Ⓓ jealous of

Word Power

Choose the English word from the Vocabulary list that correctly matches the definition.

 a process of changing from one form to another
_____

 closed in, with no escape
_____

 to brag
_____

 to pull or draw someone or something toward yourself or toward itself
_____

A Magical Evening

Skill Overview

All meaningful reading needs a purpose. When readers understand the purpose for reading a particular text, they can select the appropriate reading strategies to help them meet the reading goal.

The fourth grade classes invite you to their first play of the school year. The classes have come up with a one-of-a-kind idea. The result is a musical version of the classic *Alice in Wonderland*. It was first written by Lewis Carroll in 1865. It will be performed at the children's theater this Saturday at 7 p.m.

The Parents Club will provide snacks and drinks after the play. So be smart—be there!

🎧22

Alicia, not Alice, is the main character of this **musical**. In this **version**, she dreams that she follows her cat into her bedroom **closet**. But when she enters the closet, she can't believe what she sees. It leads her into a world of **fantasy** and **adventure**. In this **magical** place, she meets talking animals and trees. She finds secret passages. And best of all, she sees all of her friends. But here, they are all animals, too! This is when the fun begins!

Members of each fourth grade class wrote **original** songs. (They got a little help from their teachers.) Students made all the colorful costumes, too. Don't miss this play! It is **directed** by Terrence Byrd. He is one of our fourth grade teachers. Terrence also performs with the Rossmoor Civic Light Opera. It is the 10th play he has directed.

Vocabulary

⭐**musical**
a play or film in which singing and dancing play an essential part

version
a form of something that differs from the original

closet
a cupboard or a small room with a door that is used for storing things, especially clothes

fantasy
a pleasant situation that you enjoy thinking about, but is unlikely to happen

adventure
an exciting thing that a person does

magical
beautiful or delightful in a way that seems removed from everyday life

original
existing since the beginning or being the earliest form of something

direct
to guide an activity

Reading Skill Comprehension Practice

Part 1

Preview the passage. Record the information that you notice while skimming the invitation.

_____
_____
_____
_____

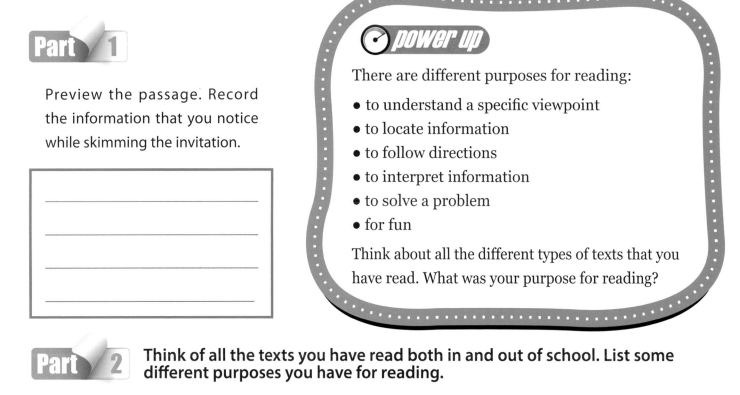

power up

There are different purposes for reading:

- to understand a specific viewpoint
- to locate information
- to follow directions
- to interpret information
- to solve a problem
- for fun

Think about all the different types of texts that you have read. What was your purpose for reading?

Part 2 Think of all the texts you have read both in and out of school. List some different purposes you have for reading.

I read to relax and to enjoy my leisure time on the weekends.

_____
_____

Part 3

1. Which would you probably reread several times? Why?

☐ a table of contents   ☐ a thank you note from a friend

Because _____
_____

2. Which might require only scanning the text? Why?

☐ a restaurant menu   ☐ directions for fixing your bike

Because _____
_____

Comprehension Review

Fill in the best answer for each question.

_____ ❶ The *main* reason to read an invitation is _____
- Ⓐ to find out where and when an event will be held.
- Ⓑ to learn how to do something.
- Ⓒ to find out someone's opinion.
- Ⓓ to find out where to buy something.

_____ ❷ Reading about the plot of the play will tell you _____
- Ⓐ when and where the play will be held.
- Ⓑ who is inviting you to the play.
- Ⓒ who will direct the play.
- Ⓓ what the play is about.

_____ ❸ You will *not* find out _____ in this invitation.
- Ⓐ where and when the play will be
- Ⓑ what time school starts
- Ⓒ who made the costumes for the play
- Ⓓ who is directing the play

_____ ❹ Why does Alicia go into her closet?
- Ⓐ She wants to get some clothes.
- Ⓑ She hears a noise in her closet.
- Ⓒ She follows her cat.
- Ⓓ She cannot find her shoes.

_____ ❺ The author wants you to _____
- Ⓐ go to the play.
- Ⓑ read *Alice in Wonderland*.
- Ⓒ try a new food.
- Ⓓ bring snacks to the play.

_____ ❻ Which question is *not* answered in this invitation?
- Ⓐ Who wrote the songs?
- Ⓑ What is the play about?
- Ⓒ Where will the play be held?
- Ⓓ How much do tickets cost?

Word Power

Choose the English word from the Vocabulary list that correctly matches the definition.

 a form of something that differs from the original

_____

 to guide an activity

_____

 an exciting thing that a person does

_____

 a pleasant situation that you enjoy thinking about, but is unlikely to happen

_____

Reading Tip

As you listen to and read the passage, think of what causes you to feel hungry.

Why You Feel Hungry

Skill Overview

Cause and effect is a text structure in which the effect happens as a result of the cause. The cause is the event or situation, and the effect is the consequence of the event or situation. The cause always happens before the effect, which leads to a result. Readers can be taught to identify this text structure to help them better understand the events in a text.

Have you ever **wondered** why you feel hungry? It's your **stomach** telling you it is time to eat. When your stomach is empty, it begins to **contract**. *Contract* means squeeze to together. There are about three contractions each minute. If you don't eat, they begin happening more often. This is your stomach sending a message to your **brain**. It is saying, "Hey! I need food down here. Hurry up!"

▲ A thermostat

The part of your brain that gives you that **empty** feeling is called the *appestat*. It is also the appestat that tells you to stop eating when you are full. No one really knows how the appestat works. Some think it may work like the thermostat in your house. When your blood is low on a fuel called **glucose**, it yells, "Time to eat!" When the glucose in your blood rises, it says, "Stop eating. You are full."

Did you know that how you feel when you eat affects the food in your stomach? If you are happy, the food is quickly **digested**. This means it is turned into fuel. If you are angry or sad, the food may just sit in your stomach. That can make you feel sick. What does this tell you? It says that it is better to be a happy eater than an angry or sad eater!

▼ Your digestive system

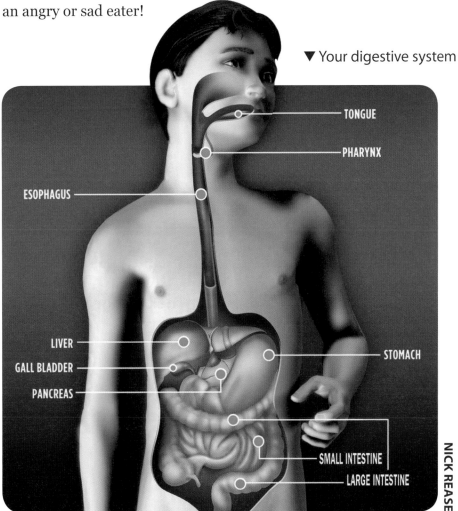

TONGUE
PHARYNX
ESOPHAGUS
LIVER
GALL BLADDER
PANCREAS
STOMACH
SMALL INTESTINE
LARGE INTESTINE

NICK REASE

Vocabulary

wonder
to ask yourself questions or wish to know about something

stomach
an organ in the body where food begins to be digested

contract
to shorten and thicken; to squeeze together

brain
the organ inside the head that controls thought, memory, feelings, and activity

empty
containing nothing

✪ **appestat**
the region of the brain that is believed to control a person's appetite for food

✪ **glucose**
a natural sugar in blood, plants, and fruits; a natural source of energy

digest
to convert into simpler forms that can be taken in by the body

93

Reading Skill Comprehension Practice

 **Write three causes and effects from the passage.**

Causes	Effects
1. You eat when you are unhappy.	1. The food may sit in your stomach.
2.	2.
3.	3.
4.	4.

Reread the passage and try to identify words indicating causes and effects. Rewrite two sentences from the passage using the example words below.

because	consequently	as a result	if	since	therefore
so	thus	for this reason	then	nevertheless	due to

1. You feel hungry because your stomach starts to contract.

2. _____

3. _____

 Please read the passage. Identify two causes from the passage that have the same effect.

Effect	
Cause	1.
	2.

94

Comprehension Review

Fill in the best answer for each question.

_____ ❶ **You feel hungry because _____**
- Ⓐ you are angry or sad.
- Ⓑ your stomach is contracting.
- Ⓒ the glucose in your blood is rising.
- Ⓓ you are digesting food.

_____ ❷ **A rising glucose level in your blood causes you to _____**
- Ⓐ feel full.
- Ⓑ feel hungry.
- Ⓒ have an appestat.
- Ⓓ feel sad or angry.

_____ ❸ **The effect of eating when you are happy is that _____**
- Ⓐ you start to feel sad.
- Ⓑ you feel hungry.
- Ⓒ food stays in your stomach.
- Ⓓ food is quickly digested.

_____ ❹ **When your stomach contracts, it is _____**
- Ⓐ telling your brain you are sick.
- Ⓑ full.
- Ⓒ squeezing itself together.
- Ⓓ opening up.

_____ ❺ **The _____ tells you to stop eating when you are full.**
- Ⓐ contraction
- Ⓑ appestat
- Ⓒ digestion
- Ⓓ blood

_____ ❻ **What might happen if you had no appestat?**
- Ⓐ You would not have a stomach.
- Ⓑ You would have more blood.
- Ⓒ You would not know if you were hungry.
- Ⓓ You would not digest your food.

Word Power

Choose the English word from the Vocabulary list that correctly matches the definition.

1 to shorten and thicken; to squeeze together (as in a working muscle)

_____

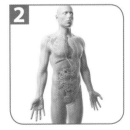

2 to convert into simpler forms that can be taken in by the body (as with food)

_____

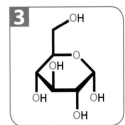

3 a natural sugar in blood, plants, and fruits; a natural source of energy

_____

4 to ask yourself questions or express a wish to know about something

_____

95

Fighting for Civil Rights

Skill Overview

A **summary sentence** summarizes the information that was covered in a passage. Summary sentences are typically the last sentence in a passage or paragraph. Effective readers are able to use summary sentences to determine main ideas and locate information.

▲ Rosa Parks is fingerprinted at the Montgomery, Alabama, police station.

GRANGER

Until 1955, it was lawyers who fought against **segregation**. To make a real difference, something big had to happen outside of the **courtroom**. On December 1, that big event took place. It was in Montgomery, Alabama.

When the buses filled up, people thought African Americans should give up their seats. Rosa Parks was an African American woman. On this day, Parks did not give up her seat to a white person. Because of this, the police put her in **jail**.

They didn't know that Parks worked with the NAACP (National **Association** for the Advancement of Colored People) in her area. A local civil rights leader named Jo Ann Robinson had a plan. She sent out flyers to every African American in their city. The **flyers** said not to ride the buses. Robinson meant for this **boycott** to last one day. Instead, it lasted one year.

This was a **peaceful protest**. No one had seen anything like this before. For the first time, it was not the lawyers fighting for African Americans' rights. It was people from all over the city. The African Americans knew that it would take all of them to change the laws.

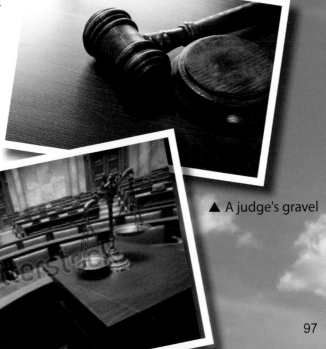

▲ A judge's gravel

▶ A courtroom

Vocabulary

✪ **segregation**
the act of separating people based on their race

✪ **courtroom**
a room where a law court meets

jail
a place for the confinement of people accused or convicted of a crime

association
a group of people organized for a joint purpose

flyer
a small piece of paper with information on it about a product or event

boycott
the practice of purposely avoiding participation in something

peaceful
without violence

protest
an organized gathering to show people's opinion against a practice, law, or idea

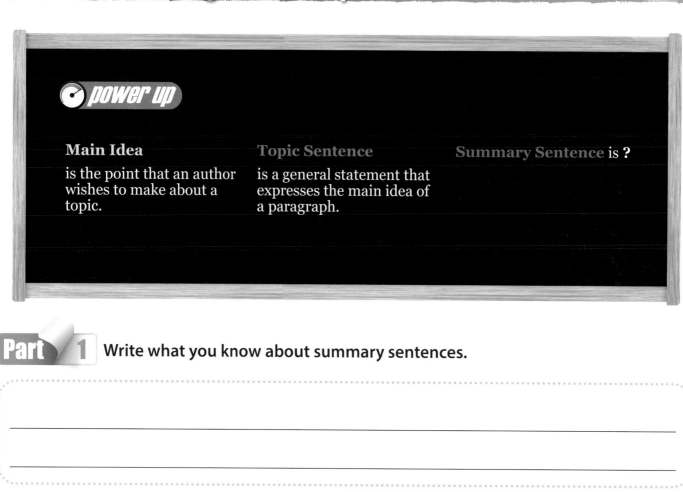

power up

Main Idea	Topic Sentence	Summary Sentence is ?
is the point that an author wishes to make about a topic.	is a general statement that expresses the main idea of a paragraph.	

Part 1 Write what you know about summary sentences.

Part 2 Write the summary sentence from this passage.

Part 3 Write the main idea of the passage.

Comprehension Review

Fill in the best answer for each question.

_____ **1** Which gives a hint about the main idea of this passage?

Ⓐ It was in Montgomery, Alabama.

Ⓑ Because of this, the police put her in jail.

Ⓒ On December 1, that big event took place.

Ⓓ The flyers said not to ride the buses.

_____ **2** Which sentence would be a good summary of this passage?

Ⓐ African Americans knew they would have to work together.

Ⓑ The Montgomery bus boycott was the first big fight for civil rights outside of the courtroom.

Ⓒ Rosa Parks was put in jail.

Ⓓ The Montgomery bus boycott was planned by Rosa Parks.

_____ **3** "*A local civil rights leader named Jo Ann Robinson had a plan.*"

Which detail does *not* go with this summary sentence?

Ⓐ Until 1955, it was lawyers who fought against segregation.

Ⓑ She sent out flyers to every African American in their city.

Ⓒ The flyers said not to ride the buses.

Ⓓ Robinson meant for this boycott to last one day.

_____ **4** "*No one had seen anything like this before.*"

What was so different about the Montgomery bus boycott?

Ⓐ For the first time, Rosa Parks was able to ride a bus.

Ⓑ It was the first time people rode buses in Montgomery.

Ⓒ For the first time, it was not just lawyers fighting for civil rights.

Ⓓ It was the first time that lawyers fought for civil rights.

_____ **5** How did Jo Ann Robinson tell people about her plan?

Ⓐ She called everyone she knew.

Ⓑ She went to people's houses.

Ⓒ She did a TV commercial.

Ⓓ She sent out flyers.

_____ **6** Rosa Parks probably_____

Ⓐ wanted to change the laws.

Ⓑ was not interested in civil rights.

Ⓒ rode the bus during the boycott.

Ⓓ did not know she was supposed to give up her seat.

Word Power

Choose the English word from the Vocabulary list that correctly matches the definition.

 **1** an organized gathering to show people's opinion against a practice, law, or idea

_____

 **2** the act of separating people based on their race

_____

 **3** the practice of purposely avoiding participation in something

_____

 **4** a group of people organized for a joint purpose

_____

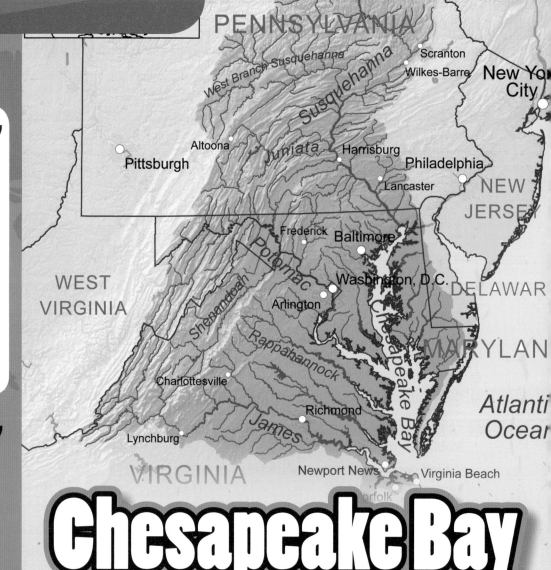

Reading Tip

 In this lesson, you are going to practice retelling. Please pay attention when reading each of the paragraphs. Read the instructions in Part 1 before listening to and reading the first two paragraphs of this passage.

Vocabulary

bay
an inlet of a body of water

locate
to be in a particular place

★**sightsee**
to go about seeing sights of interest

★**coastal**
positioned on, or relating to, the coast

★**wetland**
land consisting of marshes or swamps; saturated land

Chesapeake Bay

Skill Overview

Retelling information in a text means to put an author's words into one's own words. This allows readers to repeat ideas in an original way, which helps them deepen their understanding of what has been read.

Chesapeake **Bay** is a beautiful place where the water meets the land. It is **located** in the eastern United States. It is a large bay surrounded by Maryland, Virginia, and the Atlantic Ocean. People come from all over to sail, fish, and **sightsee** there.

But the bay is more than a great vacation spot. It is also home to some of the most famous **coastal wetlands** in the world. The long, ragged coast of the Chesapeake Bay is perfect for wetlands. Fingers of water push inland from the bay. They constantly feed the wetlands and the animals and plants living there.

The Chesapeake Bay coast

THE CHESAPEAKE BAY PROGRAM

Wetlands have running freshwater.

RICK NEASE

There are many plant and animal **habitats** in the Chesapeake Bay. One of the largest habitats is the wetlands. In wetlands, plants and animals live both above and below the water. There are different kinds of wetlands. Some have mainly trees with a few bushes. Others have mainly grasses and bushes with a few trees. Chesapeake Bay has both kinds of wetlands.

What makes an area a wetland? There are some key features. The first is, of course, the water. Wetlands have **shallow** water. The freshwater wetlands of the Chesapeake Bay are just a few feet deep. The tidal wetlands can be shallow or deep. This depends on the tides.

Wetlands are home to certain kinds of plant life. The plants are able to live in water and wet soils all year long. When the plants and trees die, they fall into the water and begin to **decay**. Animals, insects, and bacteria use the decaying material for food.

The animals of the wetlands also are able to live in the conditions there. Their bodies help them move and live in the water.

Vocabulary

habitat
place where certain plants or animals naturally or normally live and grow

shallow
not deep

decay
to rot or decompose through the action of bacteria and fungi

An egret finds food in the shallow water

THE CHESAPEAKE BAY PROGRAM

Reading Skill Comprehension Practice

Part 1 Listen to and read the first two paragraphs of the passage. Try to retell what you have learned by writing on the blank lines below. After recording this information, listen to and read the next two paragraphs.

Part 2 After reading the third and fourth paragraphs, retell what you have learned and write it on the lines below. Then listen to and read the last two paragraphs.

Part 3 After reading the last two paragraphs of the passage, retell what you have learned below.

Comprehension Review

Fill in the best answer for each question.

_____ **1** Which gives the best description of where Chesapeake Bay is located?
- Ⓐ Chesapeake Bay is in Maryland.
- Ⓑ Chesapeake Bay is in the middle of the Atlantic Ocean and Virginia.
- Ⓒ Chesapeake Bay is a place where people come to fish and sightsee.
- Ⓓ Chesapeake Bay is in the eastern part of the United States. It is between Maryland, Virginia, and the Atlantic Ocean.

_____ **2** Which is the best description of a _wetland_?
- Ⓐ A wetland is a place where plants and animals live both above and below the water.
- Ⓑ A wetland has plants and animals.
- Ⓒ Chesapeake Bay is perfect for wetlands because of the fingers of water.
- Ⓓ A wetland is a place near the Chesapeake Bay.

_____ **3** Which best describes what makes an area a wetland?
- Ⓐ A wetland has trees, bushes, and animals in it.
- Ⓑ In a wetland, the water is shallow and plants and animals live in the water and on the land.
- Ⓒ In a wetland, animals and plants live under the water all year long.
- Ⓓ A wetland has grasses and bushes and a few trees. They are in shallow water.

_____ **4** "_When the plants and trees die, they fall into the water and begin to decay._"
What is another word for _decay_?
- Ⓐ move
- Ⓑ rot
- Ⓒ speak
- Ⓓ blow

_____ **5** If you visited the wetlands, you probably would _not_ see _____
- Ⓐ water.
- Ⓑ animals.
- Ⓒ grasses.
- Ⓓ a desert.

_____ **6** Many of the animals of the wetlands probably _____
- Ⓐ do not like water.
- Ⓑ can swim.
- Ⓒ live on the top of a mountain.
- Ⓓ prefer the desert.

Word Power

Choose the English word from the Vocabulary list that correctly matches the definition.

 **1** an inlet of a body of water

_____

 **2** not deep

_____

 **3** places where certain plants or animals naturally or normally live and grow

_____

 **4** to be in a particular place

_____

Reading Tip

- Answer the questions in Part 1 before you listen to and read the passage.

- Read the title of the passage. Consider how a text with this title might be organized to present the information.

- Do you think this might be a nonfiction passage that gives facts about a female pharaoh? Could it be a tale about a mythical character? Could it be about something else?

HATSHEPSUT, FEMALE PHARAOH

Skill Overview

Your selection of reading material helps you set a purpose for reading. When you have a purpose for reading a particular text, you are able to focus on the content and have a better understanding of the text.

26

▲ Hatshepsut's Deir el-Bahri Temple

Many people have called Hatshepsut the great woman in Egypt's history. She lived during a time called the *New Kingdom*. Before her time, no woman had ever **ruled** Egypt.

About 1518 B.C., Thutmose I took the throne in Egypt. He and his queen had two sons and two daughters. But just one child lived to adulthood. Her name was Hatshepsut. When she was a teenager, her father died.

Hatshepsut was a strong young woman who wanted to **lead** others. She could read and write. And she liked to learn new things. She had watched her father while he ruled as **pharaoh**. Hatshepsut had her own ideas about how to make Egypt great.

Thutmose I had a young son with another wife. So, Thutmose II became the new pharaoh. He was just eight years old. For 10 years, Hatshepsut acted as his regent. A regent is a person who rules while the pharaoh is too young or ill. Hatshepsut was very strong willed and smart. She made most of the **decisions** about the nation. The **priests** and other leaders of Egypt followed her advice.

Thutmose II died young. In about 1504 B.C., Thutmose III became pharaoh. But he was just a baby. Again, Hatshepsut **served** as the regent. After about seven years, Hatshepsut made herself pharaoh. She ruled for 22 years. She built more **monuments** and works of art than any queen of Egypt. And she had ruled the most powerful **civilization** of her time.

Reading Skill Comprehension Practice

Reading texts that others recommend is another way to select reading material. If a friend liked a book, you may enjoy it also.

A book recommendation is a few sentences that tell why you like the book, but it should not reveal plot twists or surprise endings.

Part 1 Read the title of the passage. Then answer the questions below.

1. Which type of book is this likely to be?

_____

2. Are you interested in this kind of book? Why or why not?

I am very interested in this kind of book because

_____

_____

Part 2 Think about your reading habits. Then answer the questions below.

1. What kind of books do you like to read for fun?

_____

2. Who is your favorite author?

_____

3. What kind of books do you like to read to learn more about a topic?

_____

4. What kind of books might persuade you to think about an important issue?

_____

Part 3 Write your book recommendation below.

_____

_____

_____

Comprehension Review

Fill in the best answer for each question.

_____ **1** People who like to read about _____ would like this passage.
Ⓐ Egypt
Ⓑ oceans
Ⓒ math
Ⓓ sports

_____ **2** You would *not* read this if you wanted to _____
Ⓐ read about Thutmose.
Ⓑ learn about pharaohs.
Ⓒ learn what a regent is.
Ⓓ learn about pyramids.

_____ **3** This passage would *not* be a good choice for someone who likes _____
Ⓐ history.
Ⓑ reading about pharaohs.
Ⓒ poems.
Ⓓ stories about Egypt.

_____ **4** *"For 10 years, Hatshepsut acted as his regent."*
If you did not know what a __regent__ is, what could you do?
Ⓐ Say the word aloud.
Ⓑ Write the word.
Ⓒ Read the next sentence.
Ⓓ Read the title again.

_____ **5** Which happened *first*?
Ⓐ Thutmose I took the throne in Egypt.
Ⓑ Hatshepsut acted as regent.
Ⓒ Thutmose II died young.
Ⓓ Thutmose III became pharaoh.

_____ **6** Why did Thutmose II need a regent?
Ⓐ He left Egypt.
Ⓑ He did not want to be pharaoh.
Ⓒ He was too young to rule Egypt.
Ⓓ He asked for a regent.

Word Power

Choose the English word from the Vocabulary list that correctly matches the definition.

 choice made by a person or a group
_____

 an organized society of people
_____

 building, statue, etc., that serves as a tribute to an important person or event
_____

 to perform duties or services
_____

Reading Tip

- Please read each heading and make predictions in Part 1 before you listen to and read the passage.

- In most cases, simple typeface is appropriate; however, there are times when fancy typeface is useful.

- Think about when it would be appropriate to use simple typeface and when you would use fancy typeface.

Collecting Data

Skill Overview

Typeface refers to the style and size of letters. There are many font sizes and styles. Typeface includes italic, colored, and boldface print. Authors use different typefaces to organize information and emphasize important words and ideas.

Counting People

Governments get **data** about all the people who live in their countries. This data is called a *census*. **Census** data is collected every 10 years.

Census data is important. Census data helps governments learn about the size of cities and towns. This helps them plan for schools and roads. Governments can also **decide** whether cities need extra subways and buses.

Collecting the Census

Today, most people get their census forms in the mail. But some people do not mail them back. If the forms are not sent back, census workers need to get the data. They make phone calls or house visits.

Data for All

Many reports are made from census data. There are reports on **population** and **housing**. There is even data on how many students enroll in schools.

School planners use census data. They learn about their **neighborhoods** and cities. They can **predict** how many students will come to school. This data also tells them when they need to build new schools.

Even rescue workers use census data. Census data tells them how many people may need help in an emergency.

Vocabulary

government
a group of people with the authority to govern a country or state; a particular ministry in office

data
information that is collected

✪ **census**
an official count or survey, especially of a population

decide
to choose something, especially after thinking carefully about several possibilities

population
the number of people living in a place

housing
houses and apartments considered collectively

neighborhood
a district or community within a town or city

predict
to make an educated guess

Reading Skill Comprehension Practice

Part 1 Look at the heading for each section of the passage. Write a prediction about the content of the sections based on the headings.

Predictions

Section 1: **Counting People**	
Section 2: **Collecting the Census**	
Section 3: **Data for All**	

Part 2 Now that you have read the passage, write the main idea of each section.

Main Ideas

Section 1: **Counting People**	
Section 2: **Collecting the Census**	
Section 3: **Data for All**	

Part 2 Decide whether it would be best to use fancy letters or simple letters when writing the following types of text. Please choose the appropriate typeface below.

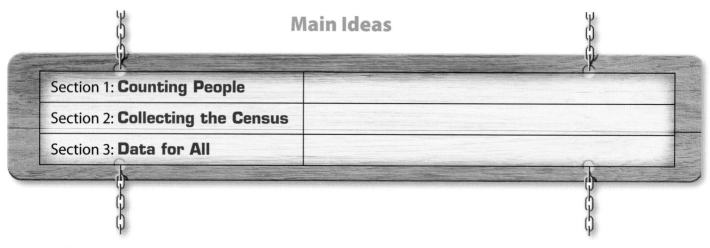

		Fancy letters	Simple letters
1.	a scientific essay	◯	◯
2.	a love letter	◯	◯
3.	a large road sign	◯	◯
4.	an invitation to a wedding	◯	◯
5.	directions for putting together a new toy	◯	◯

Comprehension Review

Fill in the best answer for each question.

_____ ❶ **Why is "*Counting People*" in large typeface?**

Ⓐ It is not important.

Ⓑ It comes before the title.

Ⓒ It is someone's first and last name.

Ⓓ It is a main idea in the passage.

_____ ❷ **Which of these is an important new term?**

Ⓐ cities

Ⓑ country

Ⓒ census

Ⓓ decide

_____ ❸ **Which is *not* an important section in this passage?**

Ⓐ Schools and Roads

Ⓑ Counting People

Ⓒ Data for All

Ⓓ Collecting the Census

_____ ❹ **Which of these can *not* be learned from census data?**

Ⓐ how many students are in school

Ⓑ where the Atlantic Ocean is located

Ⓒ the size of cities

Ⓓ how many people may need help in an emergency

_____ ❺ **Which sentence best describes why census data is important?**

Ⓐ Census data helps governments, school planners, and rescue workers.

Ⓑ Census data is important.

Ⓒ Today, most people get their census forms in the mail.

Ⓓ Census data is used so that people know where to find a bus or get on the subway.

_____ ❻ **Which statement about the census is *not* true?**

Ⓐ Census data is collected every 10 years.

Ⓑ Census data is collected by school principals.

Ⓒ Census data is used by school planners.

Ⓓ Census data is collected by forms, telephone calls, and house visits.

Word Power

Choose the English word from the Vocabulary list that correctly matches the definition.

 information that is collected

_____

 to make an educated guess

_____

 the number of people living in a place

_____

 to choose something, especially after thinking carefully about several possibilities

_____

Year-Round School

Reading Tip

There can be more than one solution to a problem.

Skill Overview

Proposition and support is a text structure in which a problem or an idea is presented and then one or more solutions are proposed. Common words are found in proposition-and-support writing and can help readers recognize this pattern.

review
to view again or to inspect

★ **readjust**
to set or adjust something again

traditional
based on custom

propose
to declare a plan for something; to suggest

model
an example to follow or imitate

★ **burn out**
to ruin one's health or become completely exhausted through overwork

improve
to get better

achievement
accomplishment

🎧 28

Summer vacation from school is too long. Students have to **review** everything in the fall when they come back to school. They have to **readjust** to the school schedule.

The **traditional** school year calendar was created when many people lived on farms. Students had the summer off so they could help with the harvesting. Now, most people do not live on farms. They do not need the whole summer off.

I **propose** that there should be more year-round schools. In this **model**, school vacations happen throughout the year. Students are still in school for the same amount of time. The vacation schedule is just spread out more. Instead of two months off in the summer, there may only be one month off. Students could still go to summer camp and have a summer vacation. Students and teachers would feel less **burned out** during the school year because their vacations would be spread out.

The research is mixed about whether year-round schools **improve** student **achievement**. Some studies show improvement, whereas others do not. Despite this, I still think the year-round school is a better model. I think it can help with the problem of the long summer vacation.

Reading Skill Comprehension Practice

Sometimes writers use key words in texts that can help readers identify a proposition-and-support pattern:

• problem	• as a result	• a reason for
• solution	• most important	• propose
• purpose	• the evidence is	• thereby

 **Write the problem addressed in this passage.**

PROBLEM

 **Think about the consequences of the problem described in the passage. Write the proposed solution to the problem.**

SOLUTION

 **Please reread the passage and circle the key words that show a proposition-and-support pattern. Then write the words on the lines below.**

Comprehension Review

Fill in the best answer for each question.

_____ ❶ *"Summer vacation from school is too long."* **What is the author's proposed solution to this problem?**

Ⓐ Students have to review everything in the fall.

Ⓑ There should be more year-round schools.

Ⓒ They have to readjust to the school schedule.

Ⓓ Students can go to summer camp.

_____ ❷ *"I propose that there should be more year-round schools."* **Which sentence does *not* support this proposition?**

Ⓐ Students and teachers would be less burned out because their vacations would be spread out.

Ⓑ Students are still in school for the same amount of time.

Ⓒ Now, most people do not live on farms.

Ⓓ Students could still go to camp and still have a summer vacation.

_____ ❸ **The author thinks that long vacations are a problem because _____**

Ⓐ students had the summer off so they could help with the harvesting.

Ⓑ many people lived on farms.

Ⓒ the vacation schedule is just spread out more.

Ⓓ students have to review everything in the fall when they return to school.

_____ ❹ **Which is a fact?**

Ⓐ The traditional school year calendar was created when many people lived on farms.

Ⓑ Summer vacation from school is too long.

Ⓒ I think it can help with the problem of the long summer vacation.

Ⓓ I propose that there should be more year-round schools.

_____ ❺ **The author wrote this passage to_____**

Ⓐ tell about farms.

Ⓑ teach you how to study.

Ⓒ get people to support year-round schools.

Ⓓ get you to go on vacation.

_____ ❻ **Students used to need the whole summer off because _____**

Ⓐ their families did not want them at home.

Ⓑ they had to study more during the summer.

Ⓒ they wanted to go on long vacations.

Ⓓ they helped with harvesting on the farms.

Word Power

Choose the English word from the Vocabulary list that correctly matches the definition.

accomplishment

_____

based on custom

_____

to declare a plan for something; to suggest

_____

an example to follow or imitate

_____

Reading Tip

One way to summarize text and find the main ideas and supporting details is to answer the "5 Ws and H" questions. However, all of the questions may not be answered and some may have more than one answer.

▼ danseur

Ballet

Skill Overview

A **summary** is a short statement, usually composed of several sentences, that covers the main idea of a passage and highlights the most important details.

Long, long ago, the first true ballet was **performed** in France. Ballet is a type of dance. It is performed with special body **movements**. It usually tells a story. Ballet began in Italy. But the first ballet school was in France. And all the words used in ballet are French. The French turned ballet into the beautiful art form we know today.

Girls who dance are called *ballerinas*. Boys who dance are called *danseurs*. They are very **athletic**. Ballet dancers may begin their **training** with classes at the age of three or four. They are introduced to music. They are taught the basic positions of ballet. By age 11 or 12, ballet dancers may have daily lessons. They must work very hard. Some dancers have a lot of **desire** and **talent**. They may be lucky enough to join a **professional** ballet company. They usually do this by age 17 or 18, or even later.

Even during their free time, ballet dancers have ballet on their minds. They are truly athletic. They always want to be strong and fit. They love that ballet gives them control over their bodies. It lets them move and **pose** in ways that are very difficult for people who are not ballet dancers.

Vocabulary

perform
to complete acts for an audience

movement
a change of position

athletic
strong, healthy, and good at sports

training
the regular practice of a skill or discipline

desire
to want or wish for something

talent
a natural ability to be good at something, especially without being taught

professional
related to work that needs special training or education

pose
to hold the body in a special position

◄ ballerina

Reading Skill Comprehension Practice

 **Part 1** Please answer the "5 Ws and H" questions. Remember, there may be more than one answer. Pick the answer you think is most important.

Questions	Answers
1. **WHO** are the dancers that perform ballet?	
2. **WHAT** is ballet?	
3. **WHERE** did ballet begin?	
4. **WHEN** do most people start to learn ballet?	
5. **WHY** do they keep practicing ballet?	
6. **HOW** does someone become a ballet dancer?	

Part 2 A passage can have more than one main idea, and a main idea can be stated in different ways. Write a main idea of this passage.

Part 3 Use your notes from Parts 1 and 2 to write a summary of the passage. Remember, a summary describes a main idea along with a few important details. Small details should not be included.

Comprehension Review

Fill in the best answer for each question.

_____ **❶ Which is a the best summary of the first paragraph?**

Ⓐ Ballet began in Italy. It became an art form in France, where the first ballet school was set up.

Ⓑ Ballet uses French words because it is a beautiful art form.

Ⓒ The first true ballet was performed in France.

Ⓓ Ballet is a kind of dance that is an art form. It began in Italy.

_____ **❷ Which list best summarizes what many ballet dancers do?**

Ⓐ learn the basic positions of ballet; use French words; tell a story

Ⓑ practice every day; go to France; tell a story

Ⓒ go to Italy; use French words; learn an art form

Ⓓ begin training at three or four; learn about music; learn the basic positions; take daily lessons

_____ **❸ Which statement best describes why ballet dancers are truly athletic?**

Ⓐ They have a lot of free time.

Ⓑ They are strong and fit and have good control over their bodies.

Ⓒ They can do things that are difficult for other people.

Ⓓ Girls are called _ballerinas_, and boys are called _danseurs_.

_____ **❹ Ballet dancers probably _____**

Ⓐ are lazy.

Ⓑ do not like being athletic.

Ⓒ are healthy.

Ⓓ have a lot of free time.

_____ **❺ What is the _first_ thing that ballet dancers do?**

Ⓐ They join professional ballet companies.

Ⓑ They begin training at age three or four.

Ⓒ They have daily lessons.

Ⓓ They end their lessons at age 17 or 18.

_____ **❻ Which is _not_ important for ballet dancers?**

Ⓐ swimming every day

Ⓑ hard work

Ⓒ practice

Ⓓ staying fit

Word Power

Choose the English word from the Vocabulary list that correctly matches the definition.

1 to complete acts for an audience

_____

2 the regular practice of a skill or discipline

_____

3 to hold the body in a special position

_____

4 strong, healthy, and good at sports

_____

Skill Overview

Questions can be asked before, during, and after reading. Questioning throughout the process is an important skill that keeps readers actively engaged. It is a strategy that helps readers understand what they have read and promotes critical thinking.

The Woodpecker and the Lion

**From *More Jataka Tales*
Retold by Ellen C. Babbitt**

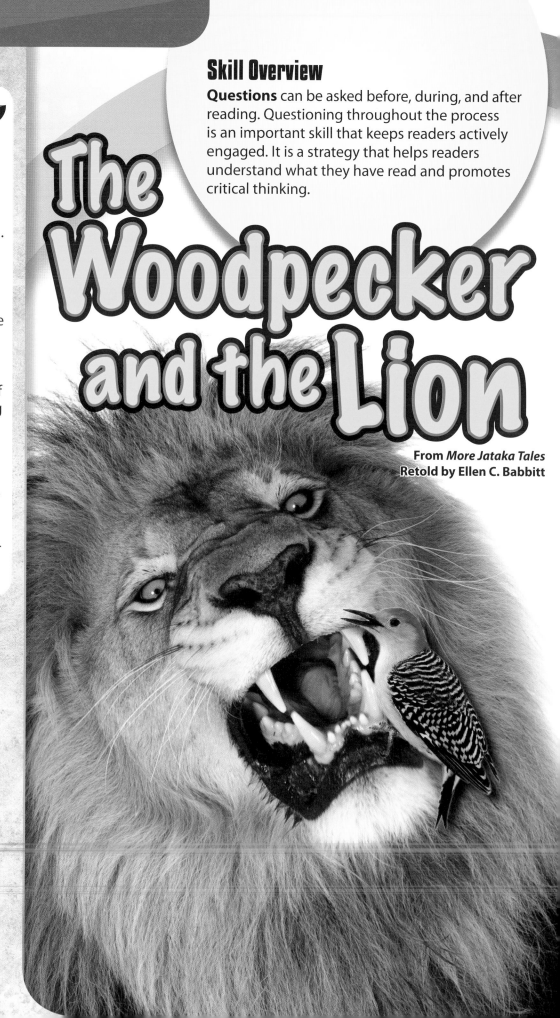

One day while a lion was eating his dinner, a bone stuck in his throat. It hurt so much that he could not finish his dinner. He walked up and down, up and down, **roaring** with pain.

A woodpecker **perched** on a branch of a tree nearby and, hearing the lion, she said, "Friend, what **ails** you?" The lion told the woodpecker what was wrong, and the woodpecker said, "I would take the bone out of your throat, friend, but I do not **dare** to put my head into your mouth, for fear I might never get it out again. I am afraid you might eat me."

"O, woodpecker, do not be afraid," the lion said. "I will not eat you. Save my life if you can!"

"I will see what I can do for you," said the woodpecker. "Open your mouth wide." The lion did as he was told, but the woodpecker said to herself, "Who knows what this lion will do? I think I will be careful."

So, the woodpecker put a **stick** between the lion's upper and lower jaws so that he could not shut his mouth. Then the woodpecker **hopped** into the lion's mouth and hit the end of the bone with her **beak**. The second time she hit it, the bone fell out. The woodpecker hopped out of the lion's mouth and hit the stick so that it would fall out, too. The lion could now shut his mouth. At once, the lion felt much better, but he did not say one word of thanks to the woodpecker.

One day later in the summer, the woodpecker said to the lion, "I want you to do something for me."

"Do something for you?" said the lion. "You mean you want me to do something more for you. I have already done a great deal for you. You cannot **expect** me to do anything more for you. Do not forget that once I had you in my mouth, and I let you go. That is all you can ever expect me to do for you."

The woodpecker said no more, but she kept away from the lion from that day on.

Vocabulary

roar
to make a long, loud, deep sound

perch
to sit on top of something

☆**ail**
to make one unwell

dare
to be brave enough to do something difficult or dangerous

stick
a thin piece of wood or other material

hop
to jump on one foot or to move about from place to place

beak
the hard, pointed part of a bird's mouth

beak ▲

expect
to think or believe something will happen or someone will arrive

Part 1 Write two questions about the first three paragraphs. Answer them if you can.

1	**Question**	What ailed the lion?
	Answer	The bone, which stuck in the lion's throat.
2	**Question**	
	Answer	
3	**Question**	
	Answer	

Part 2 After reading the next two paragraphs, please answer the questions below.

1. Do you think it was a good idea for the woodpecker to be careful?

_____

2. Did you think the lion could try to eat the woodpecker? Why or why not?

_____

Part 3 Write two questions about the end of the passage (last three paragraphs). Answer them if you can.

1	**Question**	Why didn't the lion want to do the woodpecker a favor?
	Answer	Because he believed that he had already done so by not eating the woodpecker.
2	**Question**	
	Answer	
3	**Question**	
	Answer	

Comprehension Review

Fill in the best answer for each question.

❶ _"Friend, what ails you?"_
Which correctly answers this question?

Ⓐ The lion was lost.
Ⓑ The lion hurt his paw.
Ⓒ The lion could not find food.
Ⓓ The lion had a bone in his throat.

❷ _"Then the woodpecker hopped into the lion's mouth and hit the end of the bone with his beak. The second time he hit it, the bone fell out."_
Which question do these sentences answer?

Ⓐ Where did the woodpecker live?
Ⓑ What does the lion look like?
Ⓒ How did the woodpecker get the bone out of the lion's throat?
Ⓓ How did the lion get a bone in his throat?

❸ Which question is _not_ answered in the passage?

Ⓐ What did the woodpecker want the lion to do for him?
Ⓑ How did the woodpecker help the lion?
Ⓒ How did the lion get a bone in his throat?
Ⓓ Did the lion thank the woodpecker?

❹ The woodpecker put a stick in the lion's mouth because _____

Ⓐ the lion asked him to.
Ⓑ the woodpecker used it to get the bone.
Ⓒ the lion was talking too much.
Ⓓ the woodpecker did not want to be eaten.

❺ The woodpecker probably hoped the lion would _____

Ⓐ eat him.
Ⓑ thank him.
Ⓒ roar.
Ⓓ trap him.

❻ Which word _best_ describes the woodpecker?

Ⓐ shy
Ⓑ lazy
Ⓒ clever
Ⓓ selfish

Word Power

Choose the English word from the Vocabulary list that correctly matches the definition.

1. to make one unwell

_____

2. to think or believe something will happen or someone will arrive

_____

3. to sit on top of something

_____

4. to be brave enough to do something difficult or dangerous

_____

Review Test

Questions 1–12: Read the passage. Then answer the questions that follow. Fill in the answer you think is correct.

Forces of Earth

Chapter 3: Undersea Volcanoes

Some of the biggest volcanoes on Earth have never been seen by humans. That's because they're deep under water. You'd have to dive down a mile and a half just to reach the tops of these volcanoes. This string of underwater volcanoes is called the Mid-Ocean Ridge.

The Mid-Ocean Ridge is the biggest mountain range on our planet. It's more than 30,000 miles long and almost 500 miles wide. Its hundreds of mountains and volcanoes zigzag under the ocean between the continents. They wind their way around the globe like the seam on a baseball. That means there are underwater mountains and volcanoes all around the world. Nearly every day, at least one underwater volcano erupts. Super-hot lava pours out of the volcano and onto the ocean floor.

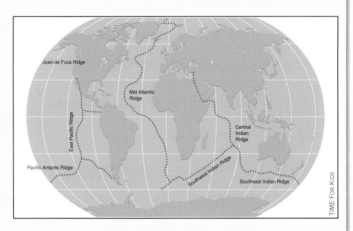

The Mid-Ocean Ridge (shown with dotted lines) winds its way between the continents like the seam on a baseball. Do you live near the Mid-Ocean Ridge?

The bottom of the sea is always changing. Super-hot lava erupts from deep inside Earth. Then the lava cools, forming rocks. Layers of rocky lava pile up. Over millions of years, all that lava makes the sea floor expand. As the sea floor expands, it pushes the continents around. A million years ago, Earth looked very different than it does today. A million years from now, it will have changed even more.

1 By previewing the passage, you can learn that it will be about _____ *Lesson 1*

- (A) mountains.
- (B) volcanoes.
- (C) animals.
- (D) the desert.

2 Which of these is another good title for this passage? *Lesson 4*

- (A) Sailing Along the Mid-Ocean Ridge
- (B) How Lava Forms
- (C) Eruptions on the Ocean Floor
- (D) The Newest Island Forms

3 Why is the sea floor constantly changing?

Lesson 23

(A) The continents get pushed around.

(B) Undersea volcanoes erupt and add lava to the sea floor.

(C) The Mid-Ocean Ridge is the biggest mountain range on our planet.

(D) Some of the biggest volcanoes on Earth have never been seen by humans.

4 Which sentence paraphrases (says the same thing as) the first paragraph?

Lesson 25

(A) The Mid-Ocean Ridge is too small to be seen by most humans.

(B) Many people have visited the Mid-Ocean Ridge.

(C) The largest volcanoes in the world are so tall that most people can't see them.

(D) Some of the largest volcanoes in the world are too far under water for most people to see them.

5 Which question is **not** answered by the passage?

Lesson 30

(A) How many continents are there?

(B) Where is the Mid-Ocean Ridge?

(C) Why is the sea floor always changing?

(D) What is the biggest mountain range on our planet?

6 What does the map show?

Lesson 14

(A) an underwater volcano erupting

(B) where the Mid-Ocean Ridge is located

(C) where New York City is located

(D) how the continents have moved

7 *Forces of Earth* is in the largest typeface because _____

Lesson 27

(A) it comes first.

(B) it is not important.

(C) it is the title.

(D) it comes last.

8 *"The bottom of the sea is always changing."*
This topic sentence tells you that the paragraph is about _____

Lesson 8

(A) swimming in the sea.

(B) how things change.

(C) seashells.

(D) how the bottom of the sea changes.

9 What does the Mid-Ocean Ridge look like?

Lesson 13

(A) the seams of a baseball

(B) a straight line

(C) a circle

(D) an ocean wave

10 *"Undersea Volcanoes"*
This chapter title helps you predict that the text is about _____

Lesson 18

(A) mermaids.

(B) volcanoes in North America.

(C) volcanoes under the ocean.

(D) building a volcano model.

11 Knowing about _____ helps you learn about volcanoes under the ocean.

Lesson 9

(A) volcanoes on land

(B) ocean waves

(C) rocks

(D) deep-sea diving

12 Which one would be a good summary of this passage?

Lesson 24

(A) There are volcanoes under the sea.

(B) A large number of underwater volcanoes are constantly changing Earth's surface.

(C) The Mid-Ocean Ridge is the biggest mountain range on our planet.

(D) There are underwater mountains and volcanoes all over the world.

Questions 13–20: Read the two passages. Then answer the questions that follow. Fill in the answer you think is correct.

Clean Up Every Neighborhood

The new president should take on the issue of pollution and how it poisons our environment. Many poisonous chemical plants and waste dumps are found in lower-income areas because people there are not involved in making decisions.

Air pollution, or smog, is caused by cars and trucks. Acid rain falls into our lakes and forests, where many fish and plants live. Many rivers and lakes are polluted with chemicals. Sounds from car traffic and airplanes cause noise pollution.

Our new president should take on these kinds of pollution first because they are affecting the lives of so many children, causing asthma, cancer, and other diseases.

Jullisa T., Grade 4

End Homelessness

There are too many homeless people who have no food, and most of them are children. Many homeless people are among the working poor. This means that they have a job, but they can't support a family or pay rent. Something else that shocked me was finding out that more than three million people are homeless at least one night during the year.

The government should educate people about the homeless. This should reduce prejudice about them. We need the U.S. government to provide programs to put people in jobs that pay well. The new president may even consider once again raising the minimum wage.

Lucas V., Grade 5

13 Which of these sentences is an opinion?

Lesson 20

(A) Many rivers and lakes are polluted with chemicals.

(B) Many homeless people are among the working poor.

(C) The government should educate people about the homeless.

(D) Air pollution, or smog, is caused by cars and trucks.

14 Which sentence supports the opinion that the government should take on the issue of pollution?

Lesson 28

(A) Pollution affects the lives of many children, causing asthma, cancer, and other diseases.

(B) The government should educate people about the homeless.

(C) The government should pass a law to protect endangered animals.

(D) Education should be the government's first priority.

15 Why did kids write these letters? Lesson 17

Ⓐ to tell why people should visit their school

Ⓑ to tell who should be the next president

Ⓒ to explain what problems the government should solve

Ⓓ to tell why they read *Time for Kids*

16 *Clean Up Every Neighborhood*

This heading tells you that the letter is about _____ Lesson 3

Ⓐ safe schools.

Ⓑ getting rid of pollution.

Ⓒ homelessness.

Ⓓ elections.

17 *End Homelessness*

This meaning clue tells you that you will read about _____ Lesson 11

Ⓐ building homes.

Ⓑ a homeless person.

Ⓒ buying homes.

Ⓓ why we should end homelessness.

18 This is a set of letters. You can predict that they will be _____ Lesson 16

Ⓐ written from one person to another.

Ⓑ recipes.

Ⓒ from textbooks.

Ⓓ a set of instructions for doing something.

19 Both letters offer ideas that will _____ Lesson 5

Ⓐ make education better.

Ⓑ clean up the environment.

Ⓒ make the country a better place.

Ⓓ make you laugh.

20 Based on the topics of these letters, you can predict that _____ Lesson 6

Ⓐ the letters will tell about travel.

Ⓑ the letters will offer ideas that are important to kids.

Ⓒ the letters will be funny.

Ⓓ the letters will offer ideas about history.

Questions 21–26: Read the passage. Then answer the questions that follow. Fill in the answer you think is correct.

The Crow and the Pitcher

Once there was a crow who was very thirsty. As he flew over the pastoral countryside, he saw an old pitcher sitting near a house.

"Maybe there's water in that pitcher!" he thought as he flew down.

The crow landed near the black and gold vessel and looked inside. There was water in it—at the bottom. He stuck his beak inside, but the pitcher was too tall. He couldn't reach the water. The sun rose high in the sky, and the crow grew even more parched.

"If I don't get some water soon, I'll die!" he croaked.

He had to get that water, but what could he do? If he turned the pitcher over, the water would run out onto the ground. He looked about, trying to think of a way to get the water. Then he saw a small pebble lying on the ground.

Suddenly, he had an idea. He picked the pebble up in his beak and dropped it in the pitcher. It made a soft plunking noise as it hit the water. He realized how nicely that would work. Quickly, he gathered more stones. One by one, he dropped them into the pitcher. Slowly, the level of the water began to rise. When it got high enough, the crow stuck his beak in the pitcher and had a long, cool drink.

The moral of this fable is: Necessity is the mother of invention!

21 What caused the water in the pitcher to rise? *Lesson 2*

- A The crow got water from a river.
- B The pitcher was tipped over.
- C The crow put pebbles in the pitcher.
- D It rained, and water fell in the pitcher.

22 Which word **best** describes the crow? *Lesson 7*

- A lazy
- B clever
- C stupid
- D jealous

23 Which one happened **last**?   Lesson 15

(A) The water in the pitcher started to rise.

(B) The crow put pebbles in the pitcher.

(C) The crow was very thirsty.

(D) The crow drank from the pitcher.

25 What was the crow's problem?   Lesson 12

(A) He was very hungry.

(B) He was lost.

(C) He was thirsty.

(D) He could not fly.

24 The crow filled the pitcher with pebbles after _____   Lesson 19

(A) he had an idea for making the water rise.

(B) the level of water began to rise.

(C) he got a long, cool drink.

(D) the water level was high enough.

26 *"He had to get that water, but what could he do?"*
If you did not know why the crow had to get the water, you could _____   Lesson 21

(A) read the title.

(B) go back and read again.

(C) read the last sentence.

(D) use a dictionary.

Questions 27-30: Read the text and look at the diagram. Then answer the questions below. Fill in the answer you think is correct.

Inside a Hurricane

The center of the storm is called the *eye*. This is a column of calm air. Powerful winds are spinning around the eye. The strongest winds form the inner wall of the eye. Giant clouds swirl around the eye. They cause large amounts of rain and lightning.

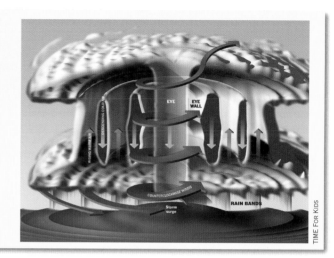

27 What happens **after** giant clouds swirl around the eye?   Lesson 10

- (A) A hurricane forms.
- (B) A column of air forms.
- (C) The winds stop.
- (D) There is a lot of rain and lightning.

29 You would read this to learn _____
Lesson 22

- (A) where to go fishing.
- (B) about our solar system.
- (C) how hurricanes form.
- (D) how to stay safe in a storm.

28 People who like _____ would probably like this.   Lesson 26

- (A) soccer
- (B) math
- (C) the desert
- (D) science

30 Which is a good way to tell someone what happens inside a hurricane?   Lesson 29

- (A) Inside a hurricane, there are powerful winds.
- (B) Hurricanes can cause damage.
- (C) The center of the storm is called the *eye*.
- (D) Powerful winds spin around the center of the storm. Clouds swirl around the center, causing rain and lightning.